Still Water

Amanda M. Kosar

Copyright © 2026 Amanda M. Kosar. All rights reserved.

"A mermaid has not an immortal soul, nor can she obtain one unless she wins the love of a human being…"
The little mermaid lifted her glorified eyes towards the sun, and felt them, for the first time, filling with tears.
—Hans Christian Andersen
"The Little Mermaid"

Part One
Loneliness

 Chapter One

The still waters were best for hunting.

Glassy surfaces emboldened the prey. Allowed them to unwind under the pretense that no harm could come from water so quiet, so clear. By the time the first hair on the back of their necks could raise in suspicion, it was always too late.

They were already hers.

In many ways, they'd always been hers, these pitiful creatures who waded through so many meaningless days only to reach that one infinitesimal moment. It was the culmination of every breath they'd ever drawn into their lungs, suspended in time and space, preparing to return to the place from whence it came. It was the moment, the one sealed with the finality of her kiss.

She filled their mouths with murky brine and their lungs with oily moss. Unseeing eyes bulged, two milky saucers spilling over with thick, yolky dribbles. Merciless darkness engulfed them, so deep, so endless, the only glimmer of light in sight was pure oblivion. And oblivion they begged for, pleading for its sweet release. She gave it to them, one last gift. Then it was over.

Finally, she could feed.

***

The sea is a lonely place, a breeding ground for solitary existences.

She was a prime specimen, however, made for those very conditions. A weapon honed over countless generations, eons of refinement and revisions to body and mind until at last the final product had been assembled. Equivocally human from the torso up, undeniably fish from the waist down.

The abyss is where she most often resided, emerging from its depths only for sustenance, something her body required remarkably little of considering she was the size of an adult woman. Delayed nutrient breakdown not only allowed her, but required her to fast for prolonged periods—typically ranging anywhere from four to six months—lest she should overfeed and put undue stress on her fine-tuned systems. Hunger was her only timekeeper, and it was now closing in, that tender emptiness in her core that told her she was primed and ready for the hunt.

Milliseconds was all it took for her body to adapt as she ascended from the deep. The nitrogen buildup in her blood from the decrease in pressure was rapidly metabolized, preventing symptoms of decompression sickness, and her pupils constricted into pinpricks to allow for the surge of light at about two hundred meters from the surface.

She cut through the water like a scythe, passing from salt into brackish into fresh water, swimming upstream through the currents of a cold river. She'd always taken a liking to the icier waters, welcoming the swell of goose pimples across the fleshy parts of her skin.

Gliding at a leisurely pace, she came to a shallow pool. There lingered the faint redolence of hot copper, a scent marked by the human life it sustained, life that she was born to take. The basin was otherwise empty.

Perhaps the people feed on the fish that nest here, she thought to herself, taking note of the small depressions in the gravel. If that were the case, then one should return in due time.

She found her own place among the hollows, using her tail to nestle in among the pebbles. They were smooth and cold against her scales.

A flash of movement in her peripheral vision. She turned to see a large gray fish positioning its tail fin on the river floor before undulating its body, a movement which sent up plumes of sediment. A new depression was left there in the gravel, fit for the fish to lay her eggs in. Seconds after expelling them from her body, her male counterpart swept in to do his duty of fertilization, after which the pair swam off as if the act had never taken place.

Alone once more, she moved closer to the nest, observing the eggs with her usual keen curiosity. A cluster of small pink orbs had adhered to the sediment just beneath the tip of her nose. She'd taken a special interest in fish eggs in the more recent years. All their various colors, sizes, and textures were so visually captivating that she simply could not resist the urge to examine them. A few times she'd even witnessed their hatching, the odd little things flittering this way and that as they came to the realization that they were now amongst the living. Some would interact with one another and others would not, but the feeling of solidarity was always there, like they somehow sensed that they'd just come from the same place. A handful of seconds like this and then they would disperse into the ocean's endless possibilities, never again to cross paths.

Eventually those very fish would grow and, one day, a man or woman might chew and swallow their slippery flesh, and the flesh of said fish would serve to nourish and replenish the flesh of man so that she might in turn eat again.

Birth, death, rebirth. Birth, death, rebirth. The song of the Sea, divine and ancient in origin.

She could feel the inexplicable kinship which existed between herself and the eggs, an invisible thread connecting them despite their vastly different places in the grand scheme of life. And so she lingered in their company for the length of her wait. Fallen into a state of waking slumber in order to preserve energy, she hadn't moved for days. Her tail was partially burrowed into the earth, allowing her to stay fixed in place while the rest of her body went soft enough to drift with the gentle currents around her. Though her appearance may have given the impression of one virtually unaware of their surroundings—an unassuming creature asleep at the bottom of the river—her acute senses were never truly put to rest.

It soon came as a subtle aroma, swirling through the water like delicate ribbons of smoke. Yes, finally, the time was nigh.

The long interval of stillness was broken at once. Dislodging her tail from the sediment, she rose soundlessly, just enough for her eyes to skim against the water's surface. It was early morning by the looks of it. The sky was coral and the air crisp. A thick layer of fog dressed the river, veiling her presence from the human that stood on the shore.

It was a small one, this human, and she seemed to exist in a state of blissful unawareness. Behind her followed a rather strange creature—a thing entirely covered in fur, scurrying to and fro on its four legs like a shell-less crab until it had worked itself into a disconcerting pant.

Unfortunately, its odor proved to be a slight obstacle in getting to the girl's, but it was of no consequence in the end. She simply had to sift through the offensive notes of hot mildew to find the scent she coveted. For a human of such small stature, the girl had an immense fragrance. The copper within her smelled savory, and the flesh sweet, like she'd been glazed with honey for the occasion. So piquant the flavors would be, so rich and inviting.

Her mouth watered until she could wait no longer.

Slowly, she waded through the water toward the shore, making herself appear as nonthreatening as possible so she might pass as a friend rather than foe. She knew that's what these small humans often sought—companionship.

The child's four-legged counterpart spotted her first, a deep rumble emitting from its pointed jaws.

"Felix, what's the matter now?" rang out the high voice of the child.

Why does a creature of the sea deign to know the language of land dwellers? It's quite simple, really. A predator must know its prey. Still, she was cautious around employing her lingual prowess, for it opened up much chance for risk. Too many times, she'd seen those much larger than herself—whales, sharks, colossal turtles—be impaled by harpoons and dragged away in nets by packs of humans. She was no fool, it was obvious that mankind could be dangerous if given the chance. Better to be quick about these things.

But this human posed no danger to her. This time there would be no need to rush.

The little one saw her then. Though they were the color of storm clouds, her eyes were clear as a summer sky. Clear and curious.

"Hello, what's your name?" the child asked.

Name? She cocked her head, trying to recall what the word meant.

"Quiet, Felix. Hush now. It's only a girl," the child scolded her infernal beast. It obeyed. "My name is Clara. What do they call you?"

Nobody had ever called her anything. At least not in the way she thought Clara meant.

"I have no name," she said, carefully forming the words. It had been long since she last spoke aloud.

"No name? Don't worry, it's okay. I can just call you Iris. That's my favorite flower, and you're pretty just like them."

Clara stuck one of her hands into a pouch that was fastened to her belt. Out came those same pudgy fingers, only now they were grasping a clump of something purple.

"These are from my garden," Clara said triumphantly.

Iris drifted toward Clara to get a closer look, wondering at the dirt caked beneath the little crescent fingernails first, then turning her attention to the flowers. There were so many of them pinched between Clara's fingers. The breeze broke a slew of petals away from their lifeless stems, whisking them up and away. Iris watched them until they disappeared.

STILL WATER

"Theo says I shouldn't keep them in here," the child said, patting her pouch. "That they'll only get crushed, but I think they're just fine. Don't you, Iris?"

The truth of the matter was that they were crushed, crushed beyond recognition, but Iris didn't know any better and neither did the girl. Iris reached out with a reluctant hand, interested to know how these bizarre fluttering things might feel to the touch. Sensing her desire, Clara extended her hand out a bit further. Soft, they were so soft, but not like the fine grains of sand that Iris often let run through her fingers. No, these were soft in the way that velvet is soft, though she had no way of making that connection herself. A small gasp escaped her at the sensation, and she withdrew her fingertips. The child giggled, still clinging to the dead flowers with the vivacity of one not yet able to understand the delicate nature of life.

"You like them," Clara observed.

Iris inclined her head in what she'd come to know as a common expression of agreement or confirmation. Then her eyes found the girl's stormy ones and there was a moment, ephemeral and short-lived, where the two smiled at each other in the way people do when they've found a shared source of joy. They might have stayed that way for a while longer if it weren't for an inopportune gust of wind, one that picked up the mouthwatering scent of the child and carried it directly to the nose of her new friend.

Perhaps if things had been different—if Iris hadn't been born a cold-hearted killer, or if young Clara had been given enough time to grow into the more skeptical mentality of one who has matured into late adolescence—perhaps then the child might have filled her pail up with water and been on her way, just as she'd intended on that chilly morning. Perhaps she and her dog might have run home and rushed through the rest of their chores, so they'd have time to play. Theo had just raked up big piles of damp black leaves the day before and, had Clara returned, he may have allowed her to romp around in them until sundown. Perhaps he may have even joined in the fun. But fate played out as it would, and sweet, naive Clara placed her unfledged trust in the woman in the water.

And so, like all the other countless poor souls, Clara was hers.

Chapter Two

A pale sliver of sunlight is what woke him. In one swift motion he tossed the tattered wool blanket from his body, groaning as the cold air assaulted his bare torso.

Four years in the Barren Crest and Theo still hadn't fully acclimated to its brutal temperatures, his mind refusing to extricate itself from memories of old. Somewhere out there still existed the balmy warmth and sunglow of the Southern Isles. It was just far, far away from here.

There, the trees had been heavily-laden with palm fronds which lived on in perpetual greenness. Here, the viridescence could be found in a rather similar abundance, but in the form of moss, lichen, and pine needles instead. And if it wasn't green, it was gray. The clouded sky above, the drapery of mist at eye-level, the dirt underfoot; it was all a drab, tenebrous blur to Theo.

He could recall a place he'd once visited as a boy, a place that made up for its deficiencies in greenness with hues of pure gold. From a distance it had seemed that the trees had all been engulfed in a blazing inferno, but the source of the shimmering colors had not been flames, but the trees' own leaves. Apparently, that was what happened when the season properly changed from summer to autumn.

Perhaps if the trees of this forest would have put on such a show, he wouldn't so much mind its unrelenting chill, but this was no such place. The deciduous trees in the region did not offer warning signs of red, orange, and yellow to signify the coming of winter. No, here winter simply came, and the trees must've understood that somehow, dropping their leaves without all the fuss.

Theo understood too, at least to some degree. Readily shedding the old to make way for the new was a concept he'd been exposed to at an age younger than most. Countries, crewmen, allies, riches—even wives. There was almost nothing that couldn't be traded in for some better alternative, at least that's what Benedict Carter would have said. It was a childish mentality which held little weight in Theo's mind anymore, for it had turned out to be the reason for his father's demise.

Four summers prior, Benedict Carter had assembled his latest and greatest crew of able-bodied men with the intent to plunder an island made of ice. They had high hopes of acquiring the land's first-rate furs and ancestral treasures, but all knew that the ice had bred a race of savage men, making for a campaign far too risky for that of a small girl, just two years of age. Consequently, a provisional cabin had been built in a secluded forest off the coast of the Castin Sea, and it was in that cabin that Theo and his cherub of a sister were to await Carter's return.

A fool to forget that a fresh crew of falsely flattering minions may not have been so trustworthy as he'd once hoped, Benedict Carter came to pay the steep price of mutiny with the thing he held most dear—his own life. And so Theo and Clara were orphaned; a mother lost to childbirth and a father lost to unchecked ambition.

But things were better this way. At least Theo thought so. Their father had been selfish and occasionally cruel, and their mother whimsically distant. It was for these reasons that Theo regarded himself a far better guardian for his sister than either of his parents had ever been.

Despite his life's constant pursuit of further land and riches, all their supposed father had been able to leave in wake of his death was the meager cabin in which they now lived. Though drafty, it was small enough to heat without much trouble, a modest fire being more than enough to make do. Positioned only half a mile west of the central vein of the Trinity River, they had access to all the drinking water they could ever need, and Theo's propensity for trapping small game meant that their stomachs remained full more often than not. On the off chance that they should want for more than the land could provide, he could make a day's journey west to the small village of Fort Zenith. There, he was usually able to locate a merchant or two passing through on their way to the Horned Isle willing to take a beaver skin or two off his hands in return for some goods or coin.

It was a fine life thus far, though Theo sometimes wondered if this was it. If he would live out the rest of his days here in this freezing forest, surviving rather than living.

To avoid such thoughts, Theo kept his mind busy with his treasured remembrances of all the endless places he had sailed to as a child. So many island towns made up of bustling, shop-lined streets. One could spend hours browsing the elaborate spreads of shoes, hats, and pants—all specially tailored to your personal measurements—before stopping into a store that sold sugar cubes, toys, and freshly cut flowers. But what he missed more than any of that were the children, children his own age that he could play with whenever he pleased. Never did he want for company during these excursions of his past, never did he feel alone.

Of course, it took some years for him to realize his father's *true* business in seeking out these charming little towns—to pilfer, slaughter, and destroy. A depraved sort of kindness it had been to allow Theo the freedom to explore each new place before stowing him in the belly of the ship so that it could be wiped off the map.

He remembered it all with great clarity. Clara, however, had been too small to remember anything beyond the Barren Crest, being but a few weeks old when their father took a new wife to replace the one who'd been too delicate to survive the child bed. There was an expeditious wedding in which Theo wore a silk waistcoat and Clara a white dress that could have belonged to a doll. Then they were whisked away at once to spend a year at sea, embarking on the voyages that would eventually bring this wife, too, to an early grave.

A fever was the culprit this time around. Within the year, they watched their father sail off for what would be his final adventure.

Clara sometimes asked about their time on the ship, but it was always as if she were asking him to tell her bedtime stories full of fantastical characters. Not as if she were asking him about her own life.

It shamed Theo to think that the entirety of his sister's experiences thus far had been confined to this little cabin, to the trees and the moss and the river, where an overly-nostalgic brother and a harebrained hound existed as her sole companions.

He cursed his miserly father, cursed him for dying his dishonorable death and leaving them so alone in this world. He longed to give Clara a life where she might go to school and make friends. Where she might behave as a proper child should.

Theo had been attempting to teach Clara her letters so that she may one day be able to read, but she seemed to struggle to understand his ways of thinking. It was apparent that he was no such teacher as the man who had taught him, and he often worried he was beginning to fail the only person in this world who depended on him. Getting his sister away from this place was his moral obligation, even if it meant skinning beavers until his fingers cracked and bled to save enough coin for safe passage out.

Theo looked over toward Clara's bedroll, unoccupied, save for the floppy doll he'd fashioned out of an empty potato sack. Felix, too, was gone. Off fetching water to use for breakfast he assumed, as they'd just ran out the night before.

It had been long since Theo traded in his linen shirts, waistcoats, and breeches for garments made of wool and tweed, materials which were far more suited for bearing the cold. He slipped into a moth-eaten shirt that billowed around his arms and a pair of long, tattered trousers before pulling on his finest article of clothing, a black long coat adorned with gold buttons. It had been his father's, and while Theo knew he'd never quite feel at home in the ostentatious thing, he couldn't deny that it provided a great deal of warmth. Lastly, he donned the soft leather boots, out of which his right big toe protruded, and then he latched the door behind him, eager to set eyes on Clara and Felix. Surely the pair of them couldn't have gotten into too much mischief so early in the morning.

The moment he set his boots on the earth Theo knew something was off, it just wasn't clear what. Damp leaves squelched beneath his every step as he went in the direction of the river, eyes scanning the perimeter for anything amiss. It was only when he paused to look over his shoulder that Theo realized his footsteps had been the *only* sound within earshot. No twittering birds, no rustling breeze, no chirping insects. Everything seemed to be preternaturally still, like the pregnant pause before a hunter releases their bowstring.

Before taking another step, he whistled. Two quick, rhythmic syllables followed by one longer one. Again. And again. The melodic phrase repeated a full four times before he paused. He held his breath as he waited to hear Clara return the call the way he'd taught her, briefly reminiscing on a time when he'd managed to successfully pass down a practical skill.

The moment he deemed Clara old enough to follow orders, Theo had sat her down to practice. Two painstakingly long days it would be before she could emulate his call.

"It's useless, Theo! I give up!" she'd pouted, plopping onto her bottom in an exaggeratedly sulky fashion.

He sat down beside her. "It took me a long time to learn too, you know. I got lost once, when I was just a little older than you are now. I was in a place I didn't know very well—woods, not unlike these. I thought I could remember which way I came, but I got all turned around and couldn't find my way back."

Clara still had her arms crossed tightly across her chest in a display of stubbornness, but Theo caught her peeking over at him as he spoke.

"The only reason I didn't stay lost for good is because Edris had taught me how to whistle on a particularly uneventful day at sea. So I stayed in one spot and whistled as loud as I could, just like Edris showed me, just like *I* am showing *you*."

"And did he find you?" Clara asked, her pout long forgotten.

Theo smiled. "He did. You take a break for now. I'm sure we'll have you singing like a little birdie in no time."

And he'd been right; she eventually had it all figured out for herself. Ever since, Theo's chest filled with pride anytime he heard her whistle, so clear and strong it was. But now he heard nothing. Not a sound. It was like the forest itself wanted to demonstrate just how absolute the absence of Clara was.

Just when he thought the building sense of dread could grow no larger without causing him to burst from within, the silence was broken by an animalistic cry.

"Felix!" Theo called, erupting into a run. The dog yelped again, a sound so panicked and desperate that it unlocked some primal instinct within him, one he'd never accessed before in his eighteen years of life.

The many roots and rocks underfoot brought him dangerously close to falling, but he didn't stop running, didn't slow down. Through the thick brush and undergrowth he tore, paying no mind to the prickling burn of the many scratches accumulating on his cheeks and hands.

He came to a screeching halt when he saw it. A man crouched down beside a snarling dog.

"*No!*" Theo's cry ruptured from somewhere deep within his chest, but he was too late. The blade had already slipped swiftly across the hound's throat.

The man turned just in time for Theo to pummel him to the ground with newfound ferocity. The element of surprise allowed him a few good blows before the man arched his weapon up and in. The

Still Water

sudden warm surge of blood coming from somewhere in his own midsection caught Theo off guard, and the man took advantage of his momentary confusion. Theo's back was now against the dirt. The entirety of the man's weight rested upon his chest, leaving him virtually incapacitated. A thick wad of bloody saliva along with a tooth or two landed beside Theo's head before the man spoke.

"The animal? It was yours?" he asked Theo, jutting his chin toward the lifeless heap of fur.

"Yes," Theo gritted out. He tried to pull his arm free so he could wipe the tear he felt rolling from the corner of his eye, but it wouldn't budge. The man applied more pressure onto Theo's wrist as if to demonstrate the futility of his struggle. He looked at him stonily through two dark eyes, nestled deeply into a face weathered by a lifetime of exposure to the elements.

During the short time in which Benedict Carter had remained in the Barren Crest, he'd warned Theo of the people who dwelled in its depths. Tree Walkers, he had called them—men and women who lived like savages up in branches so high you couldn't see them if you tried. So agile, so stealthy they were, that you wouldn't even feel it when they descended upon you and made the slit in your neck. Somewhere along the way Theo had dismissed it as a myth, invented by his father to scare him from straying too far from the cabin. But the presence of this man was making him wonder if there may have been some truth in his counsel.

"It was dying when I found it. I ended its suffering. That is all."

"Dying?" At a ripe three years of age, Felix had been healthy as a horse. Theo often made light of the dog's occasional boneheaded tendencies, but in all truth he was quite the formidable creature. Able to single-handedly kill a coyote. Faster than every rabbit they'd ever happened upon. How could a creature filled with so much life just perish this way? More importantly, how would he explain that to Clara? "What do you mean dying?"

"You've seen death before, haven't you?"

Theo wondered if he'd misheard him.

"Have I—*what*? Have I seen death? Of course I have, I'm no fledgling." His father had made him watch as diseased crew members rattled out their final breaths, required he bear witness to those who walked the plank with wrists bound in ropes. He dutifully made his compulsory appearances at countless floggings, most of which ended only when the forsaken man's glassy, unseeing eyes stared blankly ahead. He'd even seen his own mother bleed until there was no life left inside her. If Theo had become well acquainted with anything over his eighteen years, it was death.

"Then you know that when a living thing's bones have been ground into dust, they're as good as dead, even if there are still a few more breaths left in their lungs."

"What right did you have to—" Theo paused and took a breath, noticing how the branches up above were beginning to twist together in a rather hypnotic manner. He'd have to choose his next few questions carefully, while he still grasped onto the thin threads of consciousness. "What got him? A bear?"

"This was no bear," the man said.

"What, then?"

"I pray we never have to find out."

The man shifted his weight off of Theo then, towering high above him as he stood. His head whirled unnaturally with the branches of the trees.

"Wait, where is Clara? Have you seen her?"

The man said nothing, something like confusion or maybe fear passing over his features. Everything was so foggy that Theo couldn't quite discern the difference.

"Clara, she is my sister. Just a little girl. Have you seen her?"

"There was a girl along with this dog?" the man asked gravely.

"Yes," Theo said, his tone growing more urgent by the second. "Now where is she? It is time she comes home."

Still Water

He tried to sit up, tried to turn his head in hopes of spotting her golden-brown locks somewhere in the distance, but for some reason he seemed to be incapable of doing so. The man crouched down beside him and all Theo could think of was how helpless Felix must've felt in his last moments.

"I know of no girl," he said quietly, "but if she was with that dog then it is likely they shared the same fate."

Theo shook his head, still trying and failing to rise from his supine position, to keep his eyes open, to understand.

"No. No. That simply cannot be. Where is she? You've seen her, haven't you? Where is Clara?"

He had to get up now but he couldn't get his palms to grip the ground beneath him. Why was everything suddenly so slippery? Was it raining? Could that be the reason for the slickness of the dirt?

The man then laid a large, callused hand over Theo's mouth and nose and a sharp smell filled his head. "Sleep now," he heard the man say. Then he heard no more.

Chapter Three

Theo teetered in and out of reality, seeing and hearing things both real and imagined. The high trill of a birdsong, a winged maple seed twirling on an errant gust of wind, two large shining eyes gazing down upon him, the strong resonance of Clara's whistle.

Could it be? Was she truly so near? Of course she was. He never should have doubted the clever girl. He turned, exulted enough to let out a relieved laugh.

"Clara," he said, attempting to sound stern. "Don't you ever go wandering off like that ag—"

The rest of his words never had the chance to leave the gaping cavern of his mouth, for it had not been Clara who whistled, but the man. The very man who had stabbed him between the ribs and killed Felix, both without a moment's hesitation. Why was he still here? What else could he want?

Before Theo could utter a word, the man extended his arm, a marionette being tugged by an invisible string. A single grotesquely webbed claw pointed in the direction of the river. Theo noticed then that the man was sopping wet, dripping water into tranquil little puddles at his feet.

Judging by the fading light, nightfall would soon be upon them. He thought of advising the old man to seek shelter now or risk hypothermia, but something told him to remain quiet, to wait. He was right on the verge of saying something, and Theo wished to hear what it might be. But when his mouth finally opened, it was not words that spilled out, but water. On and on it poured in a torrential gush, and the more that sloshed out, the wider his mouth went, until his jaw resembled a bear trap hanging loose on its hinges.

All Theo could do was watch in horror until, finally, the last drop dribbled down the man's chin and disappeared into his scraggly gray beard. The intense eye contact they'd been maintaining was severed then, and the man's gaze followed the trajectory of his own clawed finger.

"It took her," he said.

Theo's heart leapt at that one simple word, but a mere syllable—"her." Clara.

"Who? Who took her?"

Wordless, the man continued to point.

"Please, you must tell me. You… You had mercy on my dog, and for that I thank you. Now please, extend that mercy to your fellow man. Who has taken my sister?"

His head snapped back toward Theo with a crack that sounded like the fall of a mighty oak. The man's mouth remained unmoving, but still he spoke. Or had it been a breath of wind that deposited the words in Theo's ear?

"*The Sea.*"

***

Theo awoke with a pained gasp that he half expected to flood his lungs with bubbling foam. On the ground he laid, still in the same spot the man had left him. He must've slept there in the leaves for the entire day. So many hours squandered.

Perhaps Clara had found her way back home by now, and *she* was the one fretfully awaiting her oaf of a brother's return.

With a wince, Theo moved into a seated position, grimacing as he took note of the stickiness coating his right side. He'd been wounded, that much he knew, but the only place safe enough to survey the damage was the cabin.

Clara will be there, he told himself, *she will be there waiting for you.*

Perhaps he would use the opportunity to teach her about wound care. Keeping an injury such as this clean could be the difference between amelioration and infection, between life and death. It was time she learn such lessons.

Several long minutes passed as Theo worked up the strength to rise to his feet. Then he leaned against the rough bark of a tree trunk whose diameter was triple that of his own to catch his breath. A few feet away lay the pile of fur that was Felix.

He'd almost forgotten.

One more sharp inhale, and he staggered over to him. That pathetic yelp rang through his mind like a cruel bell. It had been the poor dog's final call for help. A call that Theo had been too slow to answer.

Stooping down, he laid a hand over the wiry black fur. There was no warmth there, he observed earnestly, and he was soon forced to admit that the stolid barrier he'd attempted to erect within himself was not as fortified as he'd once hoped. As he looked down into Felix's lifeless eyes, a series of choked sobs became the battering ram that brought his composure tumbling down.

"It's all right, boy." He scooped the stiff mass of fur, flesh, and bones into his arms, outwardly numb to the sensation of his laceration igniting with fresh hot pain. "It's all right. You're only sleeping."

He repeated it to himself like a mantra.

"You're only sleeping," he said as he limped past the pool of blood he'd left behind on the forest floor.

"You're only sleeping," he whispered as he retrieved a rusty shovel from the shed.

"You're only sleeping," he grunted as he cracked through the frozen earth.

"You're only sleeping," he whimpered as he laid Felix in a shallow hole in the ground.

"You can rest now, boy. Rest well."

So weary was he by the end of the horrid act that he didn't even stop to consider how a trail of fresh blood might draw the attention of those who so greedily lap from the coursing vein of man.

***

Drunk on pain and grief, Theo had crashed into a deep sleep the moment he stepped over the cabin's threshold, unable to even make the few small steps over to his bedroll. The fragmented morning light was an intruder, stealing him away from the blissfully empty vacuum of unconsciousness.

With one eye cracked open, he began to recall all the unforeseen complications that had been dropped into his lap within the last twenty-four hours.

When he and Clara had been discarded all those four years ago, Theo was forced to trade in what was left of his beloved book collection in exchange for coin, and the time he once reserved for reading was suddenly eaten up by the endless procurement and maintenance of food, water, and shelter. After so many years living in this manner, Theo had come to consider himself rather accomplished in the art of surviving the forest. But locating a six year old girl in said forest—hundreds of acres of it—was simply not within his skill set, especially not under such mysterious circumstances.

Logic told Theo that the man in the woods had to be the culprit, for who else could it have been? Clara would not have gone past the river, and the man had obviously been well within those bounds. Furthermore, Theo had witnessed him *kill* Felix. Still, something wasn't quite right with this narrative. Felix had been maimed. Sure, a human could kill a dog like Felix with gunpowder or blades easily enough, but guns and knives could not bend all four of his limbs backwards, nor could they have left all those bite marks in his flesh. And even if a man could have somehow managed the things that had been done to Felix, he most certainly could not have accomplished it without sustaining a myriad of injuries himself. The only harm done to the man had been inflicted by Theo's fists, that much he remembered clearly.

No, the man had not mutilated Felix, which meant that he was probably telling the truth when he said he hadn't seen Clara.

So who, or what, had?

"*The Sea*," a voice seemed to whisper within the recesses of his mind, the voice from his nightmare.

He may have been mad to think this a possible lead, but the water pail was not in its usual spot beside the fireplace. He had suspected Clara had gone down to the river to begin with, and where else did the river empty itself except into the Castin Sea?

Theo peeled his shirt away from his body and ground his teeth on a strip of leather as he poured a splash of rum into his wound, washing down the sting with a sizable swig afterward. It was an angry looking gash, inflamed around the edges, but it had been inflicted near the bottom of his rib cage, hopefully sparing his lung. He was not coughing up blood, at the very least.

Ripping a strip of fabric from his shirt, he wrapped the wound tightly with intent to quell the bleeding. Cauterization was something he would very much like to avoid if at all possible.

Theo rose and stepped into the doorway to find that it had snowed sometime during the night. He stared for a moment at the pliant pine branches, all dusted with white like powdered sugar. Then he retreated back into the cabin. Near Clara's bedroll was a small chest which held her few personal possessions. Jaw clenched, Theo unlatched it and immediately found what he looked for. Her fur coat. He'd purchased it in Fort Zenith about a year ago when she finally outgrew her old woolen one.

"That's all?" he'd inquired when the merchant named his shockingly low price.

"It's but a wee thing," the merchant shrugged. "If it were a coat for you, now that'd be a different story."

Standing in the empty cabin with that very wee coat in hand, Theo had to resist the urge to look at it for fear of completely breaking. As much as he would have liked to collapse into a useless heap of heartache at that moment, he knew it was not an option. Clara was out there somewhere in the snow and she would need her coat to keep warm. He tucked it into the crook of his arm and made sure not to face in the direction of Felix's grave as he went.

He focused on his senses as he walked. The crisp air biting at the bare skin of his face, the sunlight reflecting harshly off the snow, the distant gurgle of running water, the skittering of small creatures hidden away in the brush. If he could concentrate on these things, he wouldn't have to think about what he set out to do.

It was colder at the river's edge, or perhaps he'd imagined the shiver that ran through his spine as he made the descent down the gentle slope to the water. Was it disappointment he felt when met with the same silver ribbon of water that he saw nearly every day, the same white pebbles on the ground like so many ghostly eyes looking back at him? What was it he had expected anyway? For Clara to be waiting there, an innocent smile on her face with her cheeks plump and rosy, long brown tresses neatly combed? Or had he truly anticipated finding her lifeless body, face down, gently bobbing atop the placid water like the paper boats they'd made together in years past?

Whatever the expectation might have been, there was no Clara. It was as simple as that.

Nearly ready to begin back at square one, Theo made to pivot away from the river when something glimmered in the distance. Twenty or so feet away, half buried beneath smooth pebbles, lay the metal pail. He ran to it, knees buckling when he got close enough to see its handle—the last place Clara's hand had been—and it was in that instant that Theo's entire world seemed to shatter.

"The Sea," the running water seemed to babble. *"The Sea."*

 Chapter Four

The endless stretch of horizon where sky meets sea can be a liberating sight for the many who behold its great vastness. But for any who felt as lost as Theo, it would serve as a cruel reminder of the smallness of man. It was for this reason that he most often avoided walking these weary shores, but alas, here he was.

It pained Theo to think of how his dreams of old so tremendously differed from the reality he was now living.

The deed in his coat pocket felt heavy. He'd always known of a single masted ship by the name of Black Kraken that awaited him in the Fort Zenith shipyard, but pride had caused him to spurn its existence. He thought himself too principled to accept liberation by the same hand that had immured him, but now he could see no other way. The ship purchased by Benedict Carter on a drunken whim before he left would be the one to take Theo to sea.

Theo walked against the wind, boots sinking deep into loose sand and powdery snow. His face had grown numb ages ago but his entire right side was anything but, throbbing in protest of his every step. The troubling idea that the wound still bled plagued his mind, but there was nothing to be done for it out on the empty beach anyhow. Perhaps someone in Fort Zenith would have a hand steady enough to stitch him up if need be.

For twenty long miles he stumbled down the shore, eyes fixed on the savage waves of an angry sea. Was Clara truly out there, he wondered, and if she was, how on earth was he to find her?

He pushed these thoughts aside. What he needed now more than ever was a clear mind, devoid of anything but the immediate objectives: get to the vessel and set sail. The finer details could all be worked out later.

***

"Say, what's yer business here anyway? Now hold on just a second. Are ye bleeding, boy? What the devil happened to ye?"

The energy needed to produce words had been expended long before Theo saw the first signs of the village.

"Speak up now. State yer business, I'm warning ye!"

The rising urgency in the faceless voice momentarily sharpened Theo's senses, just enough for him to notice the gun aimed directly at his chest. A surge of adrenaline allowed him one last word before he collapsed.

"Clara."

***

Pain. All Theo felt was pain. Visions of long talons ripping his torso into ribbons coursed through his mind until he could remember nothing else, until he was more so a writhing pile of raw nerve endings than man.

***

"He wake yet?" a gruff voice came from somewhere far away.

"No, still burnin' up, he is. Perhaps he'll be so lucky as to sweat out the sickness in him 'fore it spreads any further." This voice reminded him of the river, sleek and steady. It was nearly enough to beckon him to the edge of the void he'd become lost in.

"Too little, too late. Fever's got him now. Can't figure how the lad even made it to our doorstep with that nasty nick in his side. The walkin' dead if I ever did see."

Blackness again. Dark, deep, endless, like a pool of ink spilling onto a piece of parchment, it spread from all sides, stretching into the great unknown. Theo swam through it blindly, desperately grasping, though he wasn't sure what for. The awful feeling that he had forgotten something of grave importance is what pushed him to keep going when he thought he no longer could, pushed him until he could once more see light in the form of golden-brown ringlets, sparkling gray eyes, and pale freckles dappled across planes of dewy skin.

He took hold of these things and let them guide him.

***

"Yer... awake?" He recognized that voice. It was the one he had heard in the darkness, the steady one, somehow still unfaltering even through its apparent surprise. He opened his eyes to see to whom it belonged.

There was a moment where they just looked at each other, Theo and the woman, neither quite sure which of their many questions would be most proper to lead with. The woman blinked quickly. Her eyes were dark brown, like fresh mud.

"Yer awake," she said again, this time with more certainty.

Questions flailed through Theo's mind.

"Who are you?" seemed like a good place to start, or perhaps, "Where am I?" But what he found himself asking instead was, "Do you know a man by the name of Henry Stapleton?"

A crease formed between the woman's brows.

"Henry Stapleton? Why, I—" she began, and Theo could tell she was preparing to say something long-winded and irrelevant.

"I need to find Henry Stapleton," he said as if he were speaking to a simpleton.

A sharp inhalation of breath was the sole sign of her indignation before a burly grayed man made his presence known.

"What could ye possibly need with this Mr. Stapleton ye speak of?"

Theo propped himself up on his elbows to get a better view of this newcomer, emitting a strained groan as he did.

"He sold my father a boat some years ago," Theo ground out. "Where's my coat? The deed is in the pocket."

The woman made to move, probably to fulfill his request, but the older man put out a hand signaling her to stay put.

Still Water

"A boat," he said with a chuckle. "Henry Stapleton sold yer father a boat?"

"Well, it's more of a ship, really. A schooner, if I recall correctly. As I stated but a moment ago, I come with the deed in hand. It is in my coat pocket, if you'd be so good as to return it to me."

The man sat down, leaning back in his chair and crossing a pair of beefy arms over his chest. "I can guarantee ye that Henry Stapleton ain't got no ship for ye."

Theo swung his legs over the side of the bed in one quick excruciating movement. The woman cried out in alarm, standing and reaching toward him as if to assist him in lying back down. He smacked her hand away and then immediately thought better of himself.

"I'm terribly sorry," he said quickly, shame rushing through him as he met her shocked expression. "Where are my manners? I should begin by thanking you—both of you—for your hospitality and… and for the lodging." He gestured rather awkwardly to the bed and walls around him. "But I really must be going. Now if you could just point me in the direction of Henry Stapleton, I will be out of your hair once and for all."

He spotted his coat hanging on a hook on the far wall. "Ah yes, there it is. Thank you again, for everything, really." He limped pathetically across the room and then offered an equally pathetic smile to the bewildered woman and her strangely amused companion.

"Sir, yer really in no sort of shape to be—" began the woman.

"Henry Stapleton. Where would one go to find him?"

The woman rose to her feet once again, face flushed with frustration. "If ye would've had the decency to keep that damned wagglin' tongue of yers still long enough for me to get out a single word, I would've told ye right from the start that Henry Stapleton lives here, beneath this very roof! In fact, ye've been speakin' to him for the past five minutes! You ungrateful, daft, prideful ape of a man!" She threw the rag that she'd been holding in her hand to the ground and stormed out of the room, emitting a slew of curses until she could no longer be heard.

Stupefied, Theo looked back at the man, who still wore that tickled expression on his face. "Now you've gone and done it. She'll be slammin' the cupboards all night long and neither of us'll get a wink of sleep."

"You're Henry Stapleton?"

"I'm he. Work over in the shipyard, but I ain't got yer boat."

"But—"

"Let me see that deed of yers."

Theo scrambled to pull it out of the coat pocket and placed it in Henry's calloused hand. He looked down his nose at the piece of yellowing parchment, squinting his eyes and frowning in a rather dramatic manner.

"Can't read a lick of this, boy. Never learned how. But I recognize this here as my signature. The name of the ship?"

"Black Kraken."

"Ah yes, yes. I remember now. Your father… is Benedict Carter?" There was a slight edge of incredulity to his words.

Theo's mouth shrunk into a regretful line. "Yes, yes he was."

"Was? The devil got him at last, eh?" Another rotund chuckle, this one ending in a slew of wet sounding coughs. "How'd he go?" he finally managed.

"Mutiny."

Stapleton nodded. "Can't say I'm too sorry for your loss, boy."

"Nor can I."

Henry met Theo's eyes at last, clearly intrigued by his response.

"I remember the day I signed this here contract well. It'd been drawn up by a strange fellow. Southerner, I think."

"That would have been Edris, my father's first-mate. He could read and write."

"Edris, yes, that was it. A real learned man. Dead too, I presume?"

Still Water

Theo nodded, pivoting his gaze to the wall as he did so.

"Mutiny is risky business for any first-mate, 'specially a loyal one. Risky business, indeed," Henry said around the pipe in his mouth.

"You'll have to excuse my bluntness, Mr. Stapleton, but will you be able to help me or not?"

"Oh, right, right," his barreled chest convulsed with another round of painful sounding laughter. "Pardon me, my boy. It's far too easy for an old man such as myself to get swept up in times past. The ship—that's what ye be wantin' to know of. Right, of course. The Black Kraken."

"Yes, the Black Kraken," Theo urged him on. "Would you be able to bring me to it?"

"No can do. Black Kraken's gone."

"Gone?"

"Gone," Stapleton repeated with finality. "Worms got to it long before ye did. Nothin' more than driftwood now."

"So there is no ship," he said more to himself than to Henry.

It was quiet for a moment, then Henry shifted in his chair and cleared some more phlegm from his throat.

"What I said is the Black Kraken is gone. But there be scores of ships sailin' through the Fort day in and day out. Where are ye looking to go?"

Where *was* he looking to go? Now directly faced with the question, Theo realized that for all his urgency to sail away, he'd never quite decided where he planned to sail to.

"I'm... I'm looking for my sister," he said tentatively. "She's a little girl, six years of age. I was told she'd been taken to sea, and I have to find her."

"Taken to sea? By who? Pirates?"

"I do not know," he admitted.

"But what would a bunch of pirates want with a small girl like that? Unless…" Realization lit the old man's glassy eyes. Theo's heart leapt.

"Unless what?"

"Ye were quiet, weren't ye? About who yer father was?" His gaze wandered away to some distant place. "He had no shortage of enemies, that man."

Bile burned at the back of Theo's throat. Could this truly be a possibility?

"Listen now and listen good," Henry once again addressed Theo directly. "I don't claim to know very much in this life, but there's one thing I know for certain—retribution can be passed down like an inheritance. With Benedict Carter dead and gone, next in line is any poor soul that be unfortunate enough to bear his flesh and blood."

Theo looked Henry Stapleton dead in the eyes. "So what do I do?"

"Ship by the name of Cyclops will be leavin' here in one week's time. Hang 'round the harbor, make yerself useful, and pray they'll take ye on as crew. Ye can bet yer bottom dollar they'll be sailin' to Horned Isle. Most of 'em do."

"Most of who?"

"*Pirates*, of course. That's who yer looking for, ain't ye?"

All Theo could see was Clara, alone and afraid in the underbelly of some dirty pirate ship.

"Yes, I suppose it is."

Chapter Five

"I don't like the sound of it, not one bit," she scolded him as she dabbed at the wound with alcohol. "This gash of yers ain't been too kind to ye, and yer fever's yet to break."

"Perhaps if I'd have been afforded a full night's rest, I might be on the mend by now."

Henry Stapleton's daughter, Mercy, had indeed spent the better part of the night making quite the ruckus, just as her father predicted she would. A punishment well deserved Theo supposed, though he regretted that Henry, for all his graciousness, should have to endure it alongside him.

Mercy made no response, only dabbed a bit harder, earning a hiss of pain from her patient. Theo faced her with full intent to protest the roughness of her touch, but ended up just watching her instead. She had brassy blond hair, extra frizzy around her temples, and her nose was ever so slightly crooked. Her mouth was cast in a concentrated frown as she worked, forming thin lines at its corners.

"My father's a fool of a man, you know," she said after some moments passed.

"Your father is a decent and charitable man to allow me to stay here."

"Decent and charitable, yes, but no less a fool. He never should've suggested ye go and get yerself mixed up with those Cyclops heathens. A death wish is what that is."

"I think it's a fine idea given my limited options."

"Foolish," she repeated, putting the rag aside.

"Who are you to say? What knowledge have you of my situation anyhow?"

Her eyes held his own with an intensity that made him want to squirm.

"'Spose I know nothin'. Nothin' at all," she muttered, shrugging. "Best of luck to ye."

Without another word, she stood and left Theo to his own devices. He looked down at the stitches in his side, Mercy's handiwork, and was glad that he had been unconscious when she'd pulled the needle and thread through his flesh now that he'd come to know her heavy hand.

With a large exhale, he hoisted himself out of bed and pulled on his coat. The blood had been thoroughly scrubbed out, and the hole patched—not likely to be Henry's doing, Theo assumed with a twinge of guilt. He would remember to thank Mercy later, when she wasn't so cross with him.

Outside, Theo's breath formed little opaque plumes. To his right the Bromdale Mountains loomed in the distance, and to his left the Castin Sea. Straight ahead lie the dense forest that was the Barren Crest. He turned away from the trees and went left toward the harbor, which accommodated the shipyard.

It was just as much a shipyard as the decaying village of Fort Zenith was a fort. There was the seashore, of course, and then there was the open water where ships dropped anchor, and the few wood-rotted docks for row boats to moor at. Clearly it was not an elaborate shipyard that brought Fort Zenith its modest commerce, but the simple prospect of solid land and a warm meal that beckoned any respectable ship to its humble comforts.

The strong brininess in the air burned Theo's eyes as he passed by fishmonger after fishmonger. Trout, salmon, root vegetables, and pelts of all kinds were on display for sailors and villagers alike, though this so-called market seemed rather vacant, all things considered.

At one of the distant docks, Theo spied a few row boats tied off to the posts, and farther out, anchored atop a tossing sea, was the ship to which they must've belonged.

If the ship's men were not here perusing the measly stands, then where might they be? Theo turned to a stout old woman standing behind a cart piled high with dirty, shriveling potatoes.

"That ship out there, would it happen to be the Cyclops?"

"How should I know? Haven't seen none of its crew since it anchored," she scowled. "Slimy, no good drunkards."

Drunkards? Theo walked a few steps over to a particularly putrid fish stand.

"Pardon me, sir, but could you point me to the local alehouse?"

Another scowl, but at least the man had been considerate enough to swing a hand in the direction of a well-trodden path. Theo should've known that the road most traveled would be the one with a pub at its end. Sure enough, he found what he was after—a shack full of drunken sailors.

Four stood just outside the door, swaying, spitting, and mumbling incoherently, all with wooden mugs in hand. Theo slid by them without notice and into a cloud of smoke. With the wave of a hand the smoke cleared to reveal a bar and its tender, an irritable looking woman who glowered at his entry.

"Pauly, ya best get your useless behind out here. There's more of 'em a'comin'!" she screeched in the direction of what appeared to be a kitchen of some sorts. Was that a twinge of fear he heard in her voice? Theo wondered with a chill what sort of sinister arrangement the people of Fort Zenith might have with the many pirates who sailed upon its shores to avoid a looting.

Theo smiled apologetically at the woman and politely requested a single mug of ale, for that was all his coin could afford him. While waiting he took the opportunity to discreetly scan the length of the room. Men—tall and stout, thin and fat, old and young—all sat on stools or leaned against posts or stumbled to and fro. Yet the lot of them seemed to have one common trait—the rowdiness of those who recently escaped the wide open confinement of the ocean. Whether this would be advantageous or deleterious to Theo's objective was yet to be seen. On the one hand, the abundance of high spirits could mean amiability and goodwill, but it was common knowledge that men in this state had a tendency toward emotional volatility, and revelries such as this oftentimes ended in the flying of fists.

Theo's fingers had scarcely wrapped around his mug's splintered handle when he detected something out of place there within the general disorder—a lone man sitting still as stone in a shadowy corner. But it wasn't just his solitude that struck Theo as odd, it was the way this stranger's gaze seemed to already be upon him. He found himself drawn over to his eerie observer against his better judgment.

"Is this seat taken?" Theo asked.

The stranger grunted, repositioning his teeming mug closer to his end of the table, but making no move to imbibe any of its contents. Theo took that to mean he was free to sit.

"Ship's just come in, I hear."

Theo could scarcely see the stranger's face in the dimly lit alcove, but managed to catch his chin dipping in assent.

"Looks a fine ship from what I could tell. Do you happen to be a member of its crew?"

The man leaned forward into the light and Theo gracelessly choked on a swig of his ale. Glaring back at him were not *two* angry eyes, but a mere one; his left eye being no more than a glistening pink socket. Theo might have uttered some sort of apology for disturbing the man's peace and continued on his way, but he was rather preoccupied with gasping for air and spewing beer from his nose.

"No, I ain't no crew. I'm the damn captain."

Theo did all he could to cease his pathetic coughing. "*You* are the captain of the ship that sits in the harbor?"

Another dip of the chin. First Stapleton, and now this. Apparently Theo was not well versed in the way of introductions.

"I suppose I should ask if your crew is in need of another hand?" The captain went on with his glaring.

"Because... I am willing—more than willing—to offer you my services. In fact that's why I'm here at all," Theo sputtered out.

"Yer *services*? I just watched ye nearly meet yer end in a harmless mug of ale. What services do ye think ye could possibly offer me?" The captain laughed—cackled, really—and Theo shifted his weight as he waited for him to finish.

"I think that may be just a slight exaggeration, but nonetheless..." Theo muttered, clearing his throat a final time.

The captain scoffed and spread both arms wide. "Look around ye, lad! Yer surrounded by the likes of *men*. And the Cyclops, well there's a ship built for 'em. Yer but a mere boy. Weak, stupid, burdensome. All but useless to me. Now off ye go, back to yer mam's tit."

Theo's gaze darkened as he watched the captain shew him away like some commonplace pest. "I can assure you I am no boy. Let me prove my worth."

"Prove yer worth?" the captain exclaimed. "He wants to prove his worth, he does!"

Men gathered around, eyes alight with excitement. Theo stood, regarding them all with his shoulders square and chin held high.

"Lenny! Oh, Lenny boy!" the captain called out. "Where he be, the poor idiot?" He cast his yellow eye over the drove of grubby men.

Suddenly, a skinny man with a deeply pocked face was shoved to the front of the crowd. "Ah, there ye are. See, Lenny here is the lousiest of us all, and he's still more man than ye. So what'll be, then? Ye lookin' to be clobbered, boy?"

Theo had no wish to fight this man, but if it was his ticket onto the ship, then fight he must. He took one step forward and brandished his fists. The mob snickered in amusement, anticipation crackling through the air.

Theo took the initiative of making himself the aggressor and threw the first punch. It landed, but Lenny was seemingly unfazed. In fact, he even went so far as to grin a wide, toothless grin at Theo's assault, and that was when something in passive-looking Lenny's demeanor changed. He rushed at him like some sort of wild animal, head low and arms outstretched, hands gripping like claws at Theo's flesh. The pair toppled to the ground, a storm of flailing limbs. The crowd reverberated with cheers for Lenny as he tore at his opponent until, finally, there was no more struggle. When all was said and done, two men lifted Theo by the armpits and hoisted him out of the pub.

"*Theo?*" he heard Mercy's steady voice coming from some nearby place. He was tossed into cold mud before he had a chance to make sense of her presence.

Above him stood the captain, an unsettling look in his single eye. *That's the look of one who thirsts for blood*, Theo thought dazedly. It was then that he realized the captain's gaze was trained not on him, but on Mercy.

***

"So, are ye ever goin' to tell me what happened to ye, or do ye plan to just keep me wonderin'?"

Theo stole a glance at Mercy, but kept his jaw clenched shut as she passed a needle through his skin. She was re-stitching his wound where it'd come apart in the bar brawl.

"Was it a beast?" she continued. "Some teeth it must've had."

"It was no beast," Theo ground out. "But a man. A man with a blade."

Mercy's hand froze as she looked up at him. "And what'd he do that for?" Theo could see the gears turning in her mind, and he stayed quiet as she thought it through. "What were ye doin' in that awful forest anyhow?"

"Your father didn't tell you?"

"He told me very little." She returned to her prior occupation so she didn't have to see his face when she said it. "Only that ye lost a little one. Yer sister."

His heart became momentarily lodged in his throat.

"Well," he began. "Clara and I *lived* in that awful forest, but then she disappeared. I was looking for her when I was wounded. The only lead I have now is that she may have been taken to sea."

"And where'd ye get that idea?"

Theo paused, suddenly aware of how mad he must sound. "The same man responsible for this." He gestured with his chin down to his injured torso.

"Ye mean to tell me ye've been heedin' the word of someone who skewered ye like a slab of meat?" she asked incredulously. "For all ye know, *he's* the one that's got her."

"Don't you think I—" he exhaled sharply before he could lose his temper. "Mercy, I know how this all sounds, but that man did not take Clara. I had this dream, and this strong feeling afterward which seemed to pull me in that direction—toward the sea. And my dog, he was—never mind, I cannot explain to you all of the circumstances that have placed me in this position, nor would I expect you to understand them if I did. All that matters is that I get on a ship away from here, and that I do so as soon as possible. Your father says that pirates often stop here while en route to the Horned Isle."

"They do, but Theo—"

"Wherever it is that pirates go, that is where I am headed. I have reason to believe that it is they who have my sister now, and I fully intend to get her back."

Mercy was going to say something, Theo could tell, but she was interrupted by a harsh rapping at the door.

Chapter Six

"Are you expecting visitors?" Theo asked, his blood running cold.

"No," Mercy said earnestly, her voice now absent any of her usual derision for him. "Could be someone here for my father, I 'spose…" But her voice trailed off warily, doubt eating away at its edges.

She started when a second, more impatient knock sounded. An inscrutable expression fell over her face as she rose to answer it. Theo stood too, though at a significantly slower rate thanks to his various aches and pains.

Struggling to walk and pull his shirt over his head at the same time, he stumbled into place behind Mercy just in time for her to turn the knob. The hearth across the room spewed a puff of sparks as a gust of wind forced its way in, expelling what little warmth the fire had amassed.

Standing there on the threshold was the captain of the Cyclops.

"Just the two people I was hopin' to see," he said with an imposing step forward. Theo had a sinking feeling in the pit of his stomach.

"Mercy, why don't you retire to your room for a bit? I believe the captain is here to confer with me."

"Smart lad," the captain said with a piggish grin.

Mercy looked from the captain to Theo, worry plaguing the topography of her features.

"Go, Mercy. All will be well," he gently reassured her, and so reluctantly she went.

Theo kept his eyes on the captain, whose eye remained trained on Mercy as she made her retreat.

"Women are hard to come by when out at sea," the captain remarked.

"Can I help you with something, Captain?"

"Tell me yer name, son."

"Theo."

"And mine be Bartholomew. But, see, that's quite a mouthful for those who ain't got no teeth—tend to fall out when ye be confined to a ship for months on end." He smiled to show Theo two rows of blackened stubs. "So I tend to go by Bart instead. Bloody-Eye Bart."

"Captain Bartholomew, can I be of assistance or shall we both be on our way?" Theo asked coldly.

"Call me Bart, my boy." He stalked over to a chair and sat himself down on it with a labored grunt. "That's what my crew calls me."

Theo made to speak, but apparently the captain wasn't finished. "That's right. I'll take ye on, but I got just one condition. A wee favor, if ye will. Do this thing for me, and ye got yerself a guaranteed spot on the Cyclops."

Theo's eyes bore into the captain as he spoke of this so-called favor.

"And what might that be, Bart?"

"Ye and that girl of yers. The two of ye seem to be mighty friendly," he began with a lewd smirk.

"I wouldn't say that."

The captain ignored him.

"I'd even go so far as to say she trusts ye."

"I don't know what gives you that impression, Captain. I'm but a passer-through who is fortunate enough to be lodging here for a small number of days. I am not at liberty to speak to the sentiments of my hosts, but I highly doubt they'd lay very much trust in the likes of a stranger such as myself."

"Theo, ye be but a modest man. I like that about ye. But if ye seek to sail on my ship, ye'll do as I say. Tomorrow night the girl will go to the dock. I care not how ye get her there—trickery, coercion, brute force—it makes no difference to me," he shrugged. "Ah, I see it already, the hesitancy, it spreads through ye like the plague. Ye think this harmless favor I ask of ye will wound yer honor. But rest assured, Theo the Chivalrous! I don't intend no real harm to the creature. I'll simply have my way, and then yer little lassie can come right back here to the comforts of home, and we, to the sea, none the worse for it."

"I can see you've gravely misjudged my character. You'd be wise to take your leave now."

Theo was fully prepared for some sort of escalation, a sinister threat or something of the like, but the captain's self-assuredness seemed to be steadfast. He wore a snake's smile as he spoke his next words.

"No, no. Ye've misjudged yerself. I'll see ye on the morrow, ye and the girl."

With nothing left to say, the captain took his leave.

***

"No, you mustn't tell your father," Theo whispered. "It would put him in danger as well as us. Let him think the captain's visit was simply to make arrangements for my departure."

"Okay, I won't say a word of it. But what do ye plan to do?"

He thought for a moment. "I suppose I will do nothing. I should stay here for now and make certain that the foul Bloody-Eye Bastard doesn't dare to come near you."

"But then how will ye find Clara? Ye've got to board that ship, who knows how much time's left before…" her words died away. "Let me help."

Theo's eyes flashed at Mercy in astonishment. "Help? You do understand what the captain intends for you, do you not?"

"'Course I do."

"Then I cannot believe you'd make such an inconceivable assertion. It would be entirely improper. No, I will not allow it."

Mercy's eyes widened. "I didn't mean that I'd... lay with the scoundrel. How dare ye, ye blithering brute!" She smacked Theo with a startling amount of force. Then she smacked him once more for good measure.

"Ah! Okay, okay! Please, if your namesake bears any truth at all, you'll hold your hand!" Rubbing the new sore spot on his arm, he asked her, "What *do* you mean, then?"

"I mean we trick the dirty rat."

***

Theo and Mercy were as prepared as they'd ever be. He, with a sack full of ropes, his dagger, and a pilfered flintlock pistol which Mercy assured him Henry would not miss. She, with a pouch containing a small flask of rum tied around her waist.

Nerves had rendered Theo unable to eat all day. Where his apprehensions had manifested themselves in manic pacing and an upset stomach, Mercy's seemed to have the opposite effect. She was calm and quiet, meditative even. Theo wondered what she was thinking of in the hours leading up to their expedition, but he had not the courage to ask. So the only words he spoke to her were, "Mercy, it's nearly time."

She looked out the window, toward the thin crescent of orange setting over the horizon. Then she nodded stoically. He felt the need to say something else to her before they set out into the night, to assure her that everything would be fine, but knew it was a promise he could not make. So instead he asked her, "Are you sure you want to do this?"

She looked at him incredulously. "'Course I'm sure. If I wasn't, I wouldn't do it at all."

"But... I feel I must ask. Why are you helping me?"

"Because a little girl is out there somewhere, and she's in trouble. Ye seem to be the only one who has any chance of helpin' her." She said it as if it were obvious. As if anyone would risk their own neck for a child on which they had never before laid their eyes.

Something in Theo's chest squeezed tightly as Mercy turned back toward the door. His hand clasped around her wrist before he even knew what he would say, so they just looked at each other for a moment while he conjured the words.

"I forgot to thank you—for fixing the hole in my coat. So thank you for that. For everything."

"I would've done it for anyone."

He believed her wholeheartedly.

***

Bloody-Eye Bart, somehow equally repulsive in darkness as in the light of day, stood outlined by the moon's misty rays. Mercy made her approach with straight-backed conviction.

"Captain Bart, I'm told ye've requested my company on this fine evenin'."

"Fine evenin' my ass, it's colder than a gravedigger's shovel in this godforsaken place."

"Well, I got just the thing for that. This is how us mountain folk keep warm." Mercy tugged at the edges of her pouch, drawing forth the flask.

"Put that blasted thing away. I know of better ways to generate heat," Bart growled, snatching Mercy by her waist and pulling her roughly into him.

His breath was all things sour and sordid, and her entire being urged her to pull away, to cry out for help. She knew if she did Theo would emerge from his hiding spot in an instant, liberating her from these grimy, gripping hands. But then all chances of finding Clara would be squandered.

So rather than cower, Mercy tucked herself away into a quiet corner of her mind so that she could lean her body into Bart's, so that her feminine curves could press flush against his distended, old man's stomach, so that she could brush her supple lips softly against his drooping jowls and whisper into his hairy ear, "Just a small swig,

Captain, to loosen the nerves. Then we can generate all the warmth you'd like."

He produced a sound that reminded her of a grunting boar, a sickening expression on his misshapen face. "I don't drink, lass. But ye have at it, if it puts ye more at ease."

She took a single step backwards, making her eyes like a cat's as she uncorked the flask and took a long drawn sip, licking her lips so as to coat them with the bitter liquid. Then she brought those poisoned lips to Captain Bart's blackened smile, and they both fell into a deep sleep before he had the chance to defile her any further.

Now Theo rose from the brush with his sack of ropes, tying the captain's arms and legs in knots he learned as a boy. Then he positioned a sleeping Mercy in a spot he knew would be visible come daybreak, and covered her as best he could with a wool blanket. He placed a kiss of gratitude on her cheek before dragging the captain's limp body down the dock and onto the ship, where he knew a crew of men would be awaiting his return.

"You'll do well to stay where you are," Theo growled at them before they had a chance to grasp the situation at hand. He prayed they couldn't tell how the wound in his side throbbed painfully from the exertion, how his heart pounded wildly in his chest. Keeping the gun pressed to Captain Bartholomew's temple, Theo gave his orders.

"If you all do as I say, your captain shall live to see another day. If you don't, then I will blow out his brains. My request is simple. Begin sailing toward the Horned Isle."

The men stood flabbergasted, all wondering whether they should call Theo on his bluff. Upon the realization that too much time was passing, Theo jerked the gun farther into Bart's temple. There would be a nasty welt there when he woke.

"Aye, ain't ye that boy Lenny gave a proper beatin' to?" a voice inquired from somewhere within the crowd.

Theo aimed the gun inches away from Bloody-Eye Bart's foot and pulled the trigger before anyone else could chime in.

"Another word and I'll shoot off your captain's boot!" Theo yelled, giving everything he had to commanding the situation. "Now I don't think that Bart, here, will be too happy when he wakes with one less foot than he nodded off with. Especially not when he realizes it's because you *fools* hesitated to follow simple orders! Now sail!"

Theo maintained the wild look in his eyes until finally one man moved, and the others followed suit. Within minutes, the Cyclops was moving swiftly away from Fort Zenith.

As the crew became momentarily distracted with their work, Theo slumped beside the motionless body of the captain, placing a tentative hand on his own torso. His fingertips came back glistening with blood, but the panic he should have felt never came. He was fairly certain he would be killed long before the torn stitches could give him much grief anyhow.

These men would only follow his orders for so long, that much was clear, and the captain would likely wake in a few short hours. It would have been wise for Theo to use these brief moments of quiet to his advantage, to formulate some way in which he might avoid becoming a dead man by morning, but his thoughts were growing more muddled and confused with every passing second. One last hazy look out at the endless black waters, and he found himself drifting into a sleep as deep as the abyss below.

***

A screeching gull pulled him back to the waking world, and he sat up with a start. His gun. Where was his gun? And the captain, he was no longer beside him. Where had he gone? Theo cursed himself for having fallen asleep.

He scrambled onto unsteady feet, surprised that he'd not been bound in ropes by now. He listened but heard no voices, only the continuous lapping of water at the ship's hull and the noisy gull flying overhead. He watched the bird with weary eyes as it dove down to the ship's deck, probably to pick at some fish guts that'd been tossed aside.

That was when he saw it—a hand splayed out on the deck, its owner obscured by a large wooden crate. He waited for the hand to shoo the pesky bird away, but it did no such thing. Theo wondered at its uncompromising stillness, not even the slightest twitch of a finger with the hungry gull so near.

With no one else in sight, he felt he had no choice but to creep over and see what explanation he could glean for himself. Revelation came in the form of blood, so much blood that buckets could have been filled with it. Theo leaned over the ship's edge and emptied the contents of his stomach. Each step he took thereafter revealed corpse after broken corpse. The horizon was flat and desolate all around; no ships or land in sight. What living thing could have been capable of doing what had been done to these men?

Not one creature breathed the breath of life on the Cyclops that day, none but Theo himself. Out in the middle of the ocean, stranded on a vessel marked by death, he felt as if he were truly the last man on Earth.

 Chapter Seven

Theo hadn't thought to count the days, but now he wished he had. How long had he been here, laying on the splintered deck amongst the many carcasses? Not long enough for the fetor of decay to penetrate the air. Or maybe that was more so due to the cold than the passage of time.

It was so *cold*.

He licked his lips, realizing they were numb. With a trembling hand, he brushed his cheek to discover that, too, was impervious to touch. Soon he would be frozen solid, just like all the others. A hoarse laugh ripped through his throat as he considered it. Would this ship someday reach the shores of a foreign land, and if so would its people attempt to uncover what sort of tragedy had befallen its passengers? Or would an insatiable sea swallow it first? Maybe the real question should have been why he cared either way.

He could no longer look at the sky. Its endless gray seared his eyes. So he relaxed his neck and allowed his head to roll onto its right side. There was the hand again, just as he'd found it.

Theo yearned for a time when he could have assumed it belonged to a man merely sleeping off the remnants of a bottle of rum. Now it was not a hand he saw, but the sheet of frozen blood it rested upon, the broken fingers and the lacerated flesh.

He attempted to close his eyes against it, but where he longed to see blackness he saw only Felix, his body so disfigured that it no longer looked like that of a dog's. Theo's very mind had been infected, plagued by visions of death.

His stomach clenched uselessly. Apparently, his body had decided it could spare no more bile, though a part of him wished it would for the mere prospect of choking on his vomitus and ending the painfully long business that was dying.

Then, with a marked suddenness, he jolted into an upright position and miraculously *did* vomit, because the way Felix's joints had all been bent the wrong way, the way his skin had been peeled like bark from a tree, the needle-like punctures that sank down to his very bone—it was all identical to what had been inflicted upon the Cyclops's crew.

Theo heaved until he thought he'd suffocate. Then he heaved some more. So Felix and the crew seemed to have suffered the same fate, but why? At the hand of what terrible thing?

Ever since Henry put the idea in his head, Theo had been dead set on pirates. It must have been pirates behind all this madness, for who else might have had the motivation to commit such atrocities? But had that truly been the case, then where were they now? For heaven's sake, he was in the middle of the *ocean* with no land or ships in sight. When Theo had awoken on the morning of the slaughter, the bodies still had a freshness about them, not yet stiff or cold. That meant whoever had committed this sin would have had to sail in, murder the entire crew, and then sail far enough to not even be spotted on the horizon on a clear morning with virtually no wind. No ship on this earth could accomplish such a feat in so little time. The more he thought about it, the less Theo thought this could be the work of pirates.

Something about this was wrong, Theo decided. Something about *him* was wrong—yes, that was it. After all, what else did the crew and Felix have in common besides Theo's presence? How could it be that he'd happened upon the aftermath of multiple brutal murders, but never once witnessed their occurrence? Never heard the anguished cries of the dying, not even while sleeping on the very deck that they'd been butchered upon!

Theo didn't believe in superstitions or creatures of the night, content to know that the only monsters that walked the earth were in the form of man. For the first time, Theo was beginning to wonder if he might be one of them.

He did not give himself the time to decide. Instead he threw himself overboard, content to never know the answer to such a vile question.

Part Two
Infatuation

CHAPTER EIGHT

The night was thick with trickery and deceit. One human lay unconscious on the shores of Fort Zenith while another raised the sails of a stolen sea-cage. But the woman in the water cared not for the dramatics of it all. In fact, her sole reason for keeping tabs on the whole fiasco was quite simple—it concerned her upcoming meal.

Of course, Iris could not yet participate in the actual act of eating. No, it was far too early for that. Months must first pass before she would even begin to feel the next gentle prod of hunger. But just because one abstains from grazing doesn't mean they cannot play with their food.

It wasn't unheard of for Iris's kind to develop what most would call a "craving" so early on in the feeding cycle, though this would undoubtedly be her first. The idea of a long, drawn-out hunt was exhilarating to Iris. It was a thing so novel, so experimental in her eyes that it seemed as if she were on the cusp of tapping into some unlocked potential. It felt monumental.

The hull of the sea-cage pierced through the cold, black waters as Iris listened to the voices of men plotting a death. She harbored no concern whatsoever for what one human chose to inflict upon another, but it quickly became clear that it was *her* human's neck they planned to slit as he slept, and that would simply not do. It would be Iris who tore the flesh from his bones, who wet her throat with his blood. And she would not make room to share.

In an instant, she transformed herself into a seductress. With her black eyes obscured by voluptuous lashes and sharp teeth hidden beneath two sultry lips, she called out to the sailors, luring them to the rail with her song. Bewitched, the men reached for her, one or two of them preemptively plunging to their deaths without her even having to lift a finger.

Iris curved her lips, a mimicry of relief, gliding ever closer to the many outstretched hands whose fingers strained for her touch.

"Which one of you would be so kind as to help me out of this cold water?" A phrase so practiced, she need not even search for the words.

Quickly realizing they would not be able to reach her by hand alone, the men began to scurry across the deck like the simple-minded rats they were until, finally, one of them was able to procure a rope.

"Here ya go, lassie! Grab a hold of this!" he called down to her triumphantly. In all his excitement he tossed the rope over without first establishing a solid grip, and it slipped through his fat fumbling fingers, landing in the water with a splash. Iris put his face to memory. He would be the first to have his entrails plucked from his abdomen.

Within a moment the ends of multiple ropes were dangling before her, desperate voices begging her to pick theirs over all the rest. She took hold of the nearest one and was instantly pulled up through a gentle nautical breeze.

The throng of men, all ready to pounce on her the moment she came within reach, stood immobilized when Iris finally flopped onto the deck. In stunned silence they beheld what they'd so unassumingly hauled onto their ship.

The Cyclops had once been a refuge for the wanton sailor, spiriting them away from the confinements of proper society while simultaneously shielding them from the ocean's hungry maw. Their sanctuary had now been infiltrated not by a woman, but by something entirely other—a creature that would bend to the will of neither land or sea, taking both and making them her own.

Even with the tail and the claws and the teeth, none could deny the beauty that lived within her strangeness. Enchanted by the divine vision of death incarnate, not a single man was able to tear away his gaze as she opened up their bellies one by one, letting the viscera slip out and fall at their feet.

She left her human, still sleeping soundly against the mast. He hadn't even flinched during the kill. The conspirators would be left behind for him to find when he awoke, Iris's very first experience in the art of gift-giving.

She breathed in deeply, his scent alone a feast for her senses, then plunged back into the icy waters below.

 CHAPTER NINE

Iris watched with a measured gaze as a body doubled over the rail of the sea-cage, crashing into the ocean's unforgiving waves.

With arms and legs limber from the physical labor required of one who lives off the land, he should have been more than capable of keeping his head above the white caps, but he had yet to emerge from his initial plunge. Iris stayed where she was, tail oscillating to keep her in place, eyes sweeping over the swells in search of a head of brown curls.

For once, Iris found she was not confused by the actions of a human being. If anything, it made sense to her that he should leave his cage behind.

She knew that men mounted these cumbersome contraptions anytime they strayed more than a mile from the nearest coastline. They were incapable of swimming for long periods of time and even more incapable of protecting themselves while doing so. Consequently, they turned to things external, things beyond themselves which came from places of mysterious origins. That seemed to be their way.

But maybe her human had come to his senses, deciding to attempt survival through the means of his own body rather than that of a sea-cage.

It didn't take long for that small flicker of respect to shrivel into ash as she realized that his act had not been one of survival, but rather of surrender. Iris had come to know the breaking point well, that moment when the human mind shifts from clinging onto life to begging for its end. That's what he was doing. Succumbing to his weakness, the way so many humans did.

He welcomed death with open arms, and so death swam into his embrace and carried him to the shore.

She looked upon him with contempt as she laid him on the ashen sands of an island forsaken before his time. In one hand he clutched a thing that first appeared to be an animal, but upon closer inspection revealed itself to be only the fur. Humans sheathed themselves in these furs, Iris knew, but this one was much too small for the likes of her human.

He had somehow retained his grasp on it, even through the violent tides. Impressive, but unimportant. She did not care about the fur itself, but the scent held within its fibers. It still reeked of beast, but mixed in was another more piquant aroma which evoked memories of her last meal. How divine that flesh had been. So tender that it had melted on her tongue, dissolving like grains of granulated sugar. This human who lay crumpled on the sand before her now smelled strikingly similar to the one on which she reminisced. It was the very reason she'd been drawn to him in the first place, like a fish to a shiny lure.

His eyes were closed, brow creased in a subconscious effort to sputter through the water his lungs had taken in. He was alive, just barely. She pushed him onto his side, nudging him until he spewed a deluge of water. Good, at least he would not perish prematurely due to asphyxiation.

She almost left him there then, content to simply supervise from afar unless conditions warranted otherwise, but then she smelled it—the festering.

He bore a wound, fresh and putrid. That would have to be seen to soon if she wished to prevent his meat from going rancid.

So weak, so helpless he was. It was shameful. But if it was a future in which she could dine upon his flesh that she coveted, then she supposed she would have to do her part in preserving it. So she delivered him up a canal that split the island in two, leaving him in the location she deemed most well-suited to his survival.

Then she remembered a place deep below the ocean's surface, a place not far from the island, where a spindly yellow coral grew in abundance. They produced a sort of mucus, and injured dolphins often rubbed their wounds against the branches to hasten their recovery. If it could heal them, then why not a man?

As Iris weighed the possible efficacy of the coral mucus, her human's breathing progressively steadied. She returned her gaze to him, laying him once more on his back. Now that his ability to breathe had been restored, his face was no longer twisted into such an ugly scowl. Skin smooth and dewy, he almost appeared to be at peace.

Iris wondered then if sleep felt the same as death. Perhaps he had mistaken the depths of his slumber for the passage into nonexistence. Her long fingers, webbed and scaled, swept over his jaw and across his cheek, leaving dappled water droplets in their wake.

"Not yet," she whispered into the night. "Have patience, weak one."

The death you so crave will befall you soon enough.

***

Never in all his life had Theo been so cold.

His coat was so waterlogged that it seemed to weigh about fifty pounds, and his trousers and shirt clung to his shivering body. Even for one with a death wish, it was impossible to ignore the primal urge to warm himself immediately. All other things—where he was, how he still lived—would have to wait until he could lend them the proper attention, for he could not think in his current state.

The only thing that could momentarily snag his attention was Clara's coat. He did not loosen his grip on its collar despite the strong impulse to stretch his fingers to encourage the blood to flow through his cold, stiff veins.

It took a great deal of effort, but he soon managed to get himself to his feet. The sky was dark but he knew not if the night was at its end or beginning. The clouds above were wispy and translucent, like delicate sheets of chiffon draped across the moon. He couldn't make out much in the way of his surroundings, but the contour of various man-made structures in the distance was clear enough. He staggered in their direction without care for vigilance or caution. If an arrow to the chest or bullet to the brain was the customary way of greeting here, Theo would gladly accept. It made no difference to him.

Any hopes of a swift death vanished completely as he approached the nearest building—a poor excuse for a log cabin. No one lived here, at least no one who held themselves to decent standards of living.

Without thinking, Theo applied the full weight of his body to the door, foolishly expecting some resistance. It swung open and he tumbled to the floor like a man returning home after guzzling ten pints of ale. Except if this were his home, it was far from hospitable.

The floorboards were clotted with dirt and lifting in many places, and the walls were in bad shape too—the clay that once filled the gaps in between the logs disintegrating into dust. Worst of all was a sizable hole in the roof which let in a most terrible draft. But there was one thing that made up for all the cabin's faults, and that was the hearth, complete with steel and flint and enough kindling for him to start a fire.

Theo crawled over to it and struck the steel against the flint until it generated a spark. Once satisfied that the fire would not smother itself, he released his pent up breath and allowed himself to relish in the warmth of its flames. Then he undressed, hanging his wet clothes over the hearth to dry. A musty, moth-eaten blanket found thrown over a moldy bed of straw would serve well enough to warm him as long as he remained beside the fire. There, as he thawed out from nearly freezing to death, Theo fell into a fitful sleep.

The cabin's warmth had dissipated hours ago—the fire having smoldered into black embers as he slept—but Theo woke feeling feverish nonetheless. A film of sweat coated his clammy skin and he winced through the tender ache as he sat up.

The wound had been healing quite well under Mercy's care, but it was causing him a great deal of pain on this morning. The last thing he wanted was to look at it, but he could ignore it no longer.

He immediately wished he'd had the wisdom to abstain.

The scab that Mercy had worked so tirelessly to coax from his body had been torn away and replaced with the beginnings of a yellow pustule. It was infected, of that there was no doubt.

Nonetheless, he forced himself to stand and dress. In the light of day, the cabin's shortcomings were even more pronounced. It was evident from the bed and sparse furnishings that it had once been lived in, but not for a very long while. In a modest kitchen he found basic cookware and dishes, but nothing to eat or drink. Through the front window he spied a wide canal, its waters frothy and fast moving. Theo guessed that if he were to follow its current it would lead to the ocean, for he could smell the distant sea from where he stood.

Then there were the hindmost windows. These looked out onto a thicket of woods, beyond which an expansive range of rocky snow-capped mountains rose up toward the heavens. Here in the foreground were more structures like the one he'd slept within, all in the same poor condition, none of which appeared to shelter any living inhabitants.

He stepped outside. It was a settlement of some sort that he'd washed upon, one not exceedingly large in size, but enough to sustain some fifty or so men and women by the looks of it. Theo made to investigate his surroundings more thoroughly, quickly discovering that a fire must have ravaged this place at some point. Many of the standing structures were blackened and charred.

He soon located two storehouses, which had miraculously managed to remain unscathed by the flames. In one, he found lumber and a number of tools that seemed to be in working order, and in another, dry salted meats and jars of pickled vegetables. Beyond that, there was an overgrown pen that at one time likely served to confine pigs or goats, and a dilapidated structure that may have been a chicken coop. Lastly, were the thirty or so cabins in which the settlers must have slept and dressed and taken their meals.

At the point where all converged, Theo found a well. It had, by some good fortune, not yet dried up and he drank from its waters deeply, invigorating himself by wetting his face once his thirst had been quenched.

All he had seen thus far was quite standard, mundane even. Only one region thus far struck him as odd, and that was the area which belonged to the "Mourner."

The Mourner was merely an out-of-place, life-sized statue that had been erected in an arbitrary plot of dirt proximal to the canal. Theo was quite familiar with the art of sculpting from his time spent in the Southern Isles, where many artists lived and worked, drawn to the long hours of lush natural light that the region afforded them. This place, however, did not seem like the kind that would attract such talent. The days were short and the life seemed difficult, not the kind that would encourage pursuit of the arts. Yet here it stood, a disfigured woman carved into an unfamiliar type of obsidian stone, glinting hauntingly in the pale afternoon light.

From the waist up, she was completely ordinary—beautiful, even. But it was below her navel that her beauty became something more grotesque. Her legs were contorted, twisting together like one suffering through some sort of terrible metamorphosis. At their ends were not feet, but a single wide fin, the same kind that would belong to a fish. Her smooth arms were extended, as if she were reaching out for something, and her face, angelic as it was, was frozen in a perpetual state of sorrow, twisted in an unmistakable cry of despair. What may have been most unsettling were her eyes, for they were locked on what must have once been the settlement's gallows.

He soon had enough of the unnerving scene, and so he turned his back on the Mourner, vowing to avoid her anguished stare for as long as he was able.

Daylight waned with every passing moment, and Theo decided to retire to the cabin he'd slept in the night before. He would have to pilfer a few pinches of meat and maybe a jar of pickled beets to assuage the ache in his core before nightfall. In the dimness of the storehouse, he tried to predict how long he could stretch the provisions. A few weeks perhaps, if he ate sparingly.

Finally coming upon the cabin, a meager dinner in hand, Theo froze midstep.

Something waited for him there at the threshold of the door, something he could not recall leaving behind when he set out that morning.

He wondered first if he might have returned to the wrong cabin, but this question was answered by the frayed blanket draped over the windowsill. He'd hung it there to air out just after waking. It was undoubtedly the same cabin from which he had come.

"Hello?" he called out into the emptiness. "Is somebody there?"

He was answered by abundant silence.

Reluctantly, Theo made his approach, for he felt he must see what it could be that rested upon the step. His heart beat as wildly as if he were about to attempt to tame a grizzly bear. Luckily for him, this was no grizzly, but a small bushel of... *fish*? Fish and some sort of yellow gelatinous substance wrapped in a large leaf. He looked around once more, vigilant eyes calibrated to catch even the smallest semblance of movement, but everything remained preternaturally still.

With a wary hand, Theo picked up the fish and the leaf, doing his best to secure the ramshackle door behind him.

CHAPTER TEN

"Hello? Is somebody there?"

He called out in the direction of the trees, but it was from the canal that Iris watched as he poked at the fish she'd left on the step. He was apprehensive, but he took it nonetheless—the fish and the mucus, which she'd spent the better part of her afternoon carefully scraping off the surface of deep sea coral.

She waited there, eyes locked on the heap of decaying logs for a considerable stretch of time, until finally the nauseating stench of scorched fish filled the air. One cannot expect to enjoy a juicy steak without first fattening up the cow. Satisfied, Iris swam up the canal.

She'd happened upon this island by chance some time ago, long before she had any intent to use it for storing prey. Though she had brought her human here on a whim, it was proving to be ideal for her purposes thus far.

There in the deserted settlement, he could reside in one of the many unseemly land-cages that he was so accustomed to, keeping him comfortably complacent during the length of his wait, and the fact that he was the only living human on the entire island meant there would be no chance for the sea-cage incident to repeat itself. The canal was merely an added perk, granting Iris easy passage to and from her human's enclosure, allowing for easy supervision. But best of all was the fact that he could not leave. Hundreds of miles away from any of the common ship routes to the Horned Isle, he was virtually stranded, left to the will of Iris, and Iris alone.

The island had but one flaw, and that was the breathing rock. At least Iris thought it might be breathing at first glance, though it turned out not to be the case. It was by all accounts just an ordinary rock, the only odd thing about it being its remarkable resemblance to Iris herself—half woman, half fish.

For the entirety of her existence, she'd never come across any evidence to suggest she wasn't alone in this world, but then she looked into those empty eyes of stone and felt a strange sense of wonder.

Iris briefly pondered over what the rock's presence could mean for her, but in the end found the train of thought to be futile. As long as she could sense no indication of threat on the island—which she could not—then there was nothing to trouble herself about. And so she eventually put it out of her mind so that she might focus her energies on properly preparing mankind's next sacrificial lamb.

***

Theo stored away the dried meat and pickled vegetables for a later time, digging into the fish with the fervor of a starved man. Only once he'd eaten the whole of the first fish did he dare to wonder why he ate at all.

Had he not very recently attempted to put an end to all this suffering? If it was truly his desire to die, then there was no purpose in the partaking of this meal.

He should try to be objective, he knew, for there were various possibilities to consider before he could come to a true decision on matters such as his own life or death. First, there was his greatest fear—that Clara had been killed a week prior in the Barren Crest, just as Felix had. Of course he had not found her body, but it certainly could have been washed away by the slow current of the Trinity River before he arrived. Then there was the chance of her having been abducted—his original suspicion. But even if that were the case, there still remained the high probability that she was dead by now. Starvation, sickness, injury—the list of tragedies that might take the life of a captive child was virtually endless. And the heinous thought that Theo himself had somehow been responsible for her disappearance... Well, that could be dismissed as sea-crazed hysteria, could it not?

Still Water

Theo closed his eyes as if that would block his consciousness from experiencing the horrors of his mind. He steadied his breath, willing himself to focus.

If he could have confirmed with certainty that Clara no longer lived, then he would have used the kitchen knife to slit his own wrists right then and there. Regardless of all the horrid scenarios he could conjure, there was but one truth that remained—if there existed even the smallest shred of hope that Clara was still out there, still waiting for him, he had to try to find her.

Theo could not relinquish his will to live until he knew that his sister was either safe among the living or at peace in death.

So he rationalized eating the rest of the fish, and then he ate the strange paste too, which was unpleasantly bitter, and he felt better for it afterward. His wound still throbbed angrily, but his thoughts became more lucid by the minute. He would continue on his voyage to the Horned Isle in hopes of encountering any additional pieces to this haphazard puzzle. Perhaps someone there might know something he did not.

He ran his hand over the dagger that hung on his belt. He'd lost Henry's gun sometime during the chaos that had ensued on the Cyclops, but this trusty blade had been fixed to his hip since he was a boy, and it would take far more than a dip in the ocean to pry it away from him now. It was an heirloom, passed down to him by his father along with the reminder that those who hide behind the guise of friendship are often truly foe—likely the one shred of useful advice the man had ever given him.

Theo knew good and well that a single offering of fish did not mean he was free to drop his guard. His first endeavor come morning would be to attempt to fortify the cabin against any unwanted visitors, but he couldn't stop there. While security in his personal effects was indeed of great importance, his ultimate goal was to leave this place, to resume his search for his Clara. A boat would be necessary if that were to be at all possible. He would take stock of all the supplies he had at his disposal soon, but first he needed a lick of sleep.

He woke early, even before the sun, and nibbled on a bit of dried meat. The damp cold here was just as unforgiving as it was back at Fort Zenith or in the Barren Crest—perhaps even worse. He hoped to insulate the cabin against the elements, for he would require some amount of warmth in order to recover his strength for the journey ahead.

Theo began with the task of gathering lumber and tools. Naturally, he wondered why such an abundance of supplies had been left behind by his predecessors, but his suspicion was eclipsed by relief at his luck.

Ignoring the shooting protests from his wound, Theo lugged log after log from the storehouse to the cabin. By the time he was finished, he had nearly exhausted all his energy.

Sinking down onto the doorstep with a pained grimace, he regarded his progress thus far. It was not enough, nowhere near. But his hands and legs shook from overexertion and he wasn't sure he could manage much more.

With a sigh of frustration, he forced himself to break for food and water. He finished off the last bit of fish from the night before and ate the rest of the dried meat and vegetables, making a mental note that he would have to go fetch some more from the food stores before sundown. For now he closed his eyes and willed the pounding in his head to stop, though it was no use. Without his permission, sleep caught him in its clutches, a relentless pull into darkness.

He could tell the sun was well into rising before he even opened his eyes. He cursed himself for all he'd left undone the day before, then he cursed the true culprit—his wound.

It looked exactly as it felt. Terrible. Clearly, dousing it with fresh water from the well was doing it no good, and neither was nourishment. But he had important tasks to see to, and so he forced his body to move regardless of the smarting pain, vowing that he would rise and work each day until he no longer could.

Stepping out into the brittle morning air, Theo found yet another bundle of fish waiting for him. His eyes scanned the surrounding areas, combing through the straggling pines and imposing boulders, but it seemed he was alone.

The poor excuse of a door got caught in the wind then, breaking the silence with a deafening crack as it struck against the frame. The sound was a harsh reminder of just how vulnerable Theo was.

Someone had approached this door while he slept. Someone who was watching him and learning his schedule. Someone who likely had a much better lay of the land than he and was not injured or sick.

His heartbeat pounded in his ears, steady as the tick of a metronome, each foreboding beat leaving him more uncertain than the last.

Powerless to do much else, Theo endeavored to put his worries to rest, plank by plank, nail by nail.

Chapter Eleven

When it came to humans, Iris knew three things—how to find them, how to catch them, and how to kill them. Beyond that, they were rather disappointing creatures, stuck in perpetual motion to no avail. A living thing must eat, rest, and repeat; all else was superfluous, extraneous. And yet, mankind never failed to complicate things.

Her human was no exception to this rule. He had all he needed—sustenance and safety—and still he scurried about like a brainless guppy, expending every last bit of energy he acquired on strange tasks. And to make matters worse, she suspected he still hadn't tended to his wound.

Iris had left him a generous dose of mucus from the corals, and had he applied it to the affected area correctly, his overall constitution hypothetically should have improved by now. Judging by his sallow skin and unsteady gait, he had done no such thing. She must somehow provide more clarity with her next delivery of the healing balm, lest he should die within the subsequent days.

Iris watched as he clumsily teetered through the mess he'd made in front of his enclosure. With imperceptive, glassy eyes he transported tree trunks around for reasons that remained unclear to her. Then he spent a long while putting peculiar implements to use, apparently shortening some of the trunks before pounding tiny metal rods into them.

It was undeniably interesting to witness his tireless labor, even if Iris could glean no purpose from it. The only thing she'd ever worked so hard for were her meals. The more she observed, the less she thought his toils had anything to do with food, and so she could not understand why he did it at all.

Periodically, he became so winded that he had to sit to catch his breath, wiping away the perspiration that beaded up on his skin. Human sweat usually held traces of salt and steam; his now smelled of fevered rot.

At one point, he appeared to grow so flushed that he tore off his coat and unlaced his shirt, grabbing a handful of snow and smearing it over his chest. He closed his eyes and leaned his head back against a stack of logs, and it was in that motion that Iris saw he had wrapped his torso with a thick strip of fabric so as to cover the wound.

This became the catalyst for her next idea.

That night she left behind another bushel of fish and a fresh clump of coral mucus, along with a long ribbon of cotton. Now she just had to hope he was bright enough to connect the dots.

***

Theo knew his time in this world was dwindling, coming to its eventual and inevitable end.

His body was burning with sickness on the morning he found another serving of bitter yellow jelly on his doorstep. Quite similar to gulping down a thick, gelatinous apple cider vinegar, it did absolutely nothing to stir his minimal appetite. He would have discarded the stuff had he not noticed the bandage that had been left alongside it. Perhaps its taste had been so revolting because it was not meant to be taken as food, but as an ointment of sorts. Choosing to overlook the chilling fact that a stranger somehow had knowledge of his injury, Theo made one final attempt to convalesce.

The sting he felt while applying the liniment to his lesion provoked him to wonder if he might be wrong in his latest assumption. For all he knew, he was slathering himself like a biscuit with some sort of native marmalade. He almost laughed at the absurdity of the thought, but found he was too weak to produce much beyond a deranged grin.

Before he could even wrap himself with the bandage, he fell into a sleep so heavy it could easily have been mistaken for the death which had been looming so near.

***

From his shelter came no stench of cooking fish, no sound of bustling about, no sign of movement.

For days Iris waded in the canal's sloshing waters so that she might witness her human's return with her own eyes. She was tempted to slither out onto land to answer for herself whether her efforts had been wasted—if he'd succumbed once and for all—but it was an urge she resisted. Him catching sight of her and dying of fright would no more serve her purposes than if he died of rot. Besides, patience was a close companion of hers. By the time the outline of his body passed through the window at last, she felt as if she'd hardly waited at all.

When he eventually set foot outside, he appeared completely restored—skin once more supple and pink, coursing with clean blood, his gray eyes bright and full of purpose. He was the picture of health and vitality as he hefted logs up onto his shoulder and carried them to and fro.

Her delight at his survival kept her from abandoning watch. Apparently she'd become more invested in his doings than she anticipated.

Over the course of the following days, he replaced weak, rotted logs with ones new, fashioning a sort of pulley out of ropes for those that needed to be raised. Then he packed the gaps that remained in between the logs with fresh moss and thick mud. Finally, he tore down the flapping piece of wood that covered the entrance, erecting a new one in its place.

Iris now understood—he'd been attempting to fortify his cage. And that understanding led her to another rather momentous realization. Human structures did not simply spring out of thin air. No, they *made* their land-cages—and perhaps even their sea-cages—with their own hands.

Still Water

This made Iris's human and her many marine acquaintances more alike than she ever would have anticipated. One particular species of fish came to mind for their similar industrious nature. The small three-spined males would dig holes in the sand before setting out to gather algae to construct nests for their young.

She wondered then if her human built this nest in preparation for prospective offspring of his own. She did not think it likely—he had no mate to her knowledge.

Why, then? To protect *himself?* Whether that made him clever or cowardly Iris had yet to decide.

The nights passed, and with every moonrise Iris snaked her way up through snow and mud to leave her human his daily nutrient source—always a bushel of fish. During the days, when she wasn't busy fishing, she continued watching him from her usual place in the canal.

He was a creature of single-minded nature if she'd ever seen one. Whatever task it was that he endeavored to accomplish, he became entirely absorbed with it, using all his strength and ability to see it through. That was a trait she could potentially come to approve of.

After a time, it seemed he was satisfied with the improvements he had made to his own nest, but he did not clear away his materials as Iris had expected. Instead, he began working on something else. She watched diligently, interested to see what he might do next.

For the first time in her existence, the innate curiosity that had been reserved for nautical life forms alone was now being applied to a terrestrial being. Slowly, Iris progressed from loathing his strangeness to endeavoring to puzzle it out. There were so many extraordinary behaviors she had yet to understand.

One day, as Iris peeked past the edge of the canal to appreciate his latest efforts, she found herself glancing down at her own hands. She regarded her spindly, clawed fingers and the webs that stretched out between them. Had she ever used these appendages to do anything but take? Did she have any wish to?

Suddenly, Iris felt such a strong sense of disquiet that she submerged herself beneath the freezing waters and darted away, persuading herself that nightfall was nearly upon them and so she must leave to procure more fish for the following day's meal.

***

By some strange stroke of luck, Theo's wrathful wound had once again begun to scab over.

His shadow—whoever it may be that had been watching over him since he washed up on these strange shores—had given him a second chance at life, at saving his sister. The awareness that he was being watched kept him on edge, but his fear was just beginning to recede. Whether that was due to true benevolence on his shadow's behalf, or Theo's own innate desire to no longer be alone was unclear. Regardless, he made a conscious decision. He would attempt to return the favor that had been done unto him. With no knowledge of who his shadow was or what sort of gift they might appreciate, Theo settled on something universal—food.

He began by fashioning a simple snare at the outskirts of the woods. When it caught him a decent sized snowshoe hare, he set about his next task.

It had been some time since he'd been by the storehouse that accommodated the comestibles—he'd been persisting largely on fish, a most preferable alternative to the saltiness of preserved meat.

It was dark inside, the only light spilling in through the door which Theo had propped open with a large stone. The low shelf of spices on the far wall was what he sought. None of them were labeled, so he spent some time twisting open each vial and sniffing their contents, one by one. Any that smelled as if they might pair well with the hare were placed in a small pile to his right, and the others were promptly returned to the shelf. He arrived back at the cabin with his pockets full of clinking glass.

Theo had never been much for cooking but he did what he could with what he had, and upon taking a small bite he reckoned it wasn't half bad. Satisfied with his work, he wrapped the warm, tender hare in some papers procured from the storehouse and tied it up with a string of frayed twine.

As he lay on his bed of straw that night, he was surprised at how pleased he was with himself. He felt giddy, lying there in the darkness imagining his shadow's reaction upon discovering his gift. He slipped into sleep before they could arrive, but dreamed of things such as friendship and camaraderie.

Chapter Twelve

The moon waned, shining just enough to illuminate Iris's path away from the canal. Despite her naturally amphibious nature, she had always felt a strong aversion to the way dirt or sand grated upon her tail. Snow, on the other hand—that was different. She savored the cool nip on her scales, its malleability and the way it so eagerly melted at her touch to leave behind beads of water on her fingertips. It made the short trips to her human's nest all the more enticing.

Iris's nose crinkled as she made her approach on this night. It reeked strongly of dead animal. *Cooked* dead animal. Surely the fetid fumes from his dinner should have dissipated by now, so late into the night. But this foul miasma was not emanating from the hearth within his nest. No, it came from outside, on the step.

She looked down at the parcel, resisting the urge to gag. Why had he disposed of his food here in this manner? Had it spoiled? Did he simply not wish to ingest it? Though she may have found it personally repulsive, it did not smell of mold or decay. If anything, it seemed perfectly fit for human consumption.

Iris struggled to understand.

She picked it up and held it for a moment, feeling its warmth seep into her hands through the paper.

Carefully, Iris deposited her delivery of fish in its usual place before slithering back to the canal. She sank into the dark waters and spent the remainder of the night crumbling the hare's soft flesh with her fingers, watching as the opportunistic guppies pecked at it with delight.

***

Even in the midst of his youth, Theo had seldom experienced the emotion often referred to as "child-like joy." When in the presence of his father, he'd always felt a constant pressure to carry himself with reserved caution, lest he be struck on the side of the head and ordered to sharpen up. And during those rare moments in which he could relax, he typically found repose in one of Edris's many books. This made for a rather serious child, not one prone to fits of silliness or glee.

But how else could this feeling be described? His excitement was a high he'd scarcely felt before, one he had no wish to come down from. His gift had been accepted; he and his shadow had officially acknowledged each other's presence. Theo smiled without realizing it as he brought in his latest shipment of fish, placing it aside for cooking later in the day.

Over the past week or so, Theo had made considerable improvements to the cabin and drawn up some simple plans for a boat. He had all he needed to begin the build, but there was one nagging detail that would not allow him to lend the entirety of his focus to his work—he did not know where he was. How could he expect to build a vessel with the purpose of conveying himself to the Horned Isle if he did not know where he might be in relation to it? And so his plan for this day became making an attempt to regain his bearings.

Before he had so rashly thrown himself from the bow of the Cyclops, Theo's compass had pointed due west. If the currents had held strong in that direction, then it would be reasonable to believe he'd landed somewhere west of Arladia, putting the Horned Isle somewhere northeast from where he now stood. He knew he would need more than a general direction if he were to truly reach such a specific destination, but it was a start at the very least.

His speculations thus far were good and well, however there was but one inconsistency that would not allow him to press forward, and that was that the only documented landmass west of Arladia was Cyanto.

The two continents were separated by thousands of miles of open sea, a distance impossible to traverse in the amount of time Theo had been on the water. That, along with the fact that Cyanto's coastline was dotted with densely populated cities, told him that the remote shores he'd awoken on simply could not be the shores of that distant land. This could mean one of three things—he'd been in possession of a faulty compass, the tides had turned and carried him in a different direction, or he currently stood upon unmapped land.

Theo warmed his fingers with his breath as he walked the length of the canal, going in the direction of the current, following the many chunks of ice to wherever it was they went. He was in the early weeks of December by his estimation, and the temperature was likely to drop by a few more degrees come January. If Theo had any say in the matter, he would be far from this place by then, in the Horned Isle with Clara safely in tow.

This place was rocky and jagged, the canal lined with moss-clad boulders that stood taller in height than Theo himself. He noticed that in general there was a scarcity of trees here, save for the densely wooded area behind the cabin. He did not know how far those woods stretched, but had gathered that the ground beyond that region was far too lithic to host the sort of lush green forests that he'd grown accustomed to.

His thighs burned from trudging through the snow, but he welcomed the discomfort, knowing it would make him stronger for whatever might lie ahead.

Finally, the mouth of the canal opened up into a wide expanse of sea. The slate gray waters were broken by a great deal of icebergs, some large and some small, all glowing bright white in the chalky noontime light. They formed a sort of maze that would undoubtedly present difficulties when it came time for navigation, but at least he now knew in what direction the sea lay.

Still Water

Satisfied with the day's findings, Theo made his way back up the canal and to the cabin. He was tired, but felt it fit to use up the few remaining hours of daylight sawing timber into planks for the boat.

Seeing his doorstep from where he worked brought about thoughts of his shadow. Who were they? A sole survivor of a deadly plague? A bandit on the run from consequence? A man marooned on these sinister shores like himself?

Regardless of their origins, Theo felt confident that his shadow was alone. Companionless, isolated, estranged from society. He and his shadow had these things in common. If someone were to ask him why he felt this so strongly, he would have no real answer except to recall a phrase that Edris used to say from time to time.

"Birds of a feather flock together."

That was as close as he could come to an understanding of it.

Soon it grew too dark for any further work. As he retreated into the cabin, he realized with some surprise that he might like to meet his shadow; to put a face, a name, an *essence* to this abstract blank slate that existed within the confines of his imagination. Anticipation kept him from his dinner that evening. Instead, he paced over the creaky floorboards like a caged animal, waiting for his shadow to make their nightly appearance.

His plan was simple; he would delay sleep until he heard movement from beyond the door, then he would make his approach, express his gratitude for the fish and the medicine, and see where things might go from there. It was not by any means a firm plan—there was most certainly room for error, for there were so many elements that he would never have been able to predict—but it was all he had, and therefore he must content himself with it. Unfortunately, he was never granted the chance to see any part of it through, because his shadow never arrived.

He puzzled over this for the entirety of the day that followed, until finally he grasped the answer that should have been most obvious to him—his shadow did not wish to be seen. Theo had taken no measures to hide the fact that he'd been awake the night before, prowling about the cabin in the firelight with all the curtains drawn back. This person that he so desired to meet was clearly shy, and if he wanted to make their acquaintance he would do well to respect that.

As the day's watery sunlight began to fade, Theo dutifully ate his dinner and washed up, slipping into bed a bit earlier than usual. Though his eyes were shut, he willed himself to cling onto consciousness, for if he fell asleep, he would fail to achieve his objective. At the slightest semblance of a sound, he would crack open a single eye, hoping to catch even a glimpse of his shadow through the window from where he lay.

He waited for what felt like ages, peeking through his narrowed eyes for false alarm after false alarm. Wind or rustling branches or the activities of small nocturnal creatures kept alerting him, only to leave him more disappointed than the time before.

Finally, just moments before he would have been persuaded to surrender to sleep at last, he heard a thump that was so insubstantial he nearly ignored it. Nonetheless, he stealthily opened his heavy eyes in what would be his final attempt of the night. If no one was there, he would permit himself a well-deserved slumber.

It took everything in his power to remain silent when he saw it—the slight motion in the dim moonlight. His shadow had come after all! He waited patiently, praying that they might pass by his window. Just a quick glance was all he wanted, a mere silhouette would do. Anything, just to sate his curiosity for a time.

To his astonishment, his prayer was answered. His shadow crossed right by his window. *She* crossed right by his window. A woman!

He could decipher the outline of her profile, limned by balmy moonbeams. The delicate curve of a cheek, the soft bow of a lip, the gentle slant of a nose, a sheet of long, dark hair hanging loosely around her shoulders. Despite his initial assertion that he would have been entirely satisfied to see even an indistinct delineation of his most mysterious visitor, Theo now felt as if he'd been cheated.

He wished to invite her in so that he might see her more clearly beneath the firelight's waxy glow, so that he might speak to her and she to him.

So quickly she had gone, far too quickly, leaving Theo to stare blankly at the cracks in the ceiling. He would not sleep that night, not even a wink.

A simple thing, once a most trivial act—picking up a bushel of fish from his doorstep—now held such great significance to him. As he clasped his hands around the fish's cold scales the next morning, he could only imagine how her slender fingers had very recently done the same. In Theo's mind, a vague sort of connection between them formed in that moment; an intangible, incomprehensible affinity toward this woman who had gone out of her way to save the life of a stranger.

A great sense of shame overcame him as he acknowledged this simple fact—she had indeed saved his *life*, and his sole act of reciprocation thus far had been in the form of a poorly prepared dish of bony hare. In fact, he hadn't even put it on a proper dish! He'd simply wrapped it in a sheet of paper and left it out on the doorstep like he would a bone for a dog. Disgraceful—everything about it was utterly disgraceful. But if he could not take back what had already been done, he could at least try to make amends.

Theo had so much work to do, an entire boat to build and a journey over sea to prepare for, but he supposed a small portion of his evenings could be set aside for other, less important pursuits. After all, how difficult could it possibly be to procure a gift more suited to the tastes of a lady?

Chapter Thirteen

Theo was already well-versed in the art of routine from his time spent in the Barren Crest, so it was only natural that he should establish one here as well.

Each morning he would wake eagerly to retrieve his parcel of fish, after which he would settle in for a quiet meal to fuel himself for a long day of work on the boat.

He kept his mind busy with the repetition of sawing planks and nailing them together until daylight began to wear thin. Any fool could see that Theo was no shipwright, but he pushed through the minor setbacks in the early stages of the build by reminding himself he had no need for a state of the art vessel. It was simply a flotation device capable of conveying him from point A to point B that he was after.

When he wasn't engaged in work, Theo walked through the ghost town with his head down. These were the moments in which he would grant his mind a slight reprieve, allowing his thoughts to wander from planning and logistics for just a bit. Of course it never took long for the mysterious woman to cross his mind, where she existed only as a starlit silhouette.

The sun had been making an uncharacteristic appearance over the past few days, and so the snow had loosened and even melted a bit in some places, leaving spots of black dirt pockmarked throughout the white. Within these irregularly shaped holes Theo was able to spy various bits and bobs that had been temporarily unearthed—sticks, pebbles, acorns, dead leaves. He looked at the objects as though considering them for something, though he could not have said what if asked. Perhaps it was inspiration he sought while on these solitary walks.

His many years alone had left him severely out of practice in the ways of women—not that he'd ever had much practice to begin with—but he was determined to redeem himself for his initial unbefitting gift. The first two evenings he spent walking without direction, though he intentionally avoided the Mourner and her unsettling stony gaze. Anywhere outside of her domain was fair game. From the place where the pale sky met the mountaintops all the way down to the ground beneath his feet, Theo looked for something, anything that might spark even the smallest inception of an idea, yet each night he returned to the cabin with nothing in hand nor mind.

Still, whenever the moon reached its pinnacle in the indigo sky, she came, and the nights soon became the only thing that pushed Theo through the many strenuous days. He grasped onto them like a drowned man would grasp onto a rock in the midst of a tempest.

On one particular evening walk, Theo strayed from the woodlands bordering the settlement's western edge, deciding instead to take a stroll along the canal. Rotting leaves recently exhumed from their tombs beneath the snow floated atop the water, drifting in the current. He imagined them as little boats carrying miniature families to their various destinations. On one boat a man held a woman in his arms, and their rambunctious dog amused them by chasing his own tail. On another, a mother rocked a sleeping babe while a father played jacks with a young child. One further upstream bore an elderly couple who sat beside one another, hand in hand as they sailed toward the encroaching horizon. Theo sighed a great puff of air, growing more melancholic with every leaf that passed.

He stood and left abruptly, paying no mind to the direction he went in, as long as it was away from those woeful feelings. So lost in thought was he that he didn't even realize he'd nearly collided with the Mourner. There she stood on her misshapen tail, reaching out toward Theo as if to touch his cheek. He knew it was just a statue, a thing made of earth and stone, but he had the uncanny feeling that he was being watched whenever he came near it.

He shook his head and forced himself to approach the statue, to face this irrational fear of an inanimate object. As he closed the distance between them, he saw something glimmer in her outstretched hand. A pearl—the largest pearl he'd ever laid eyes on, about the size of a robin's egg, and powdery pink in color. He plucked it from her palm quickly, childishly believing her fingers might close around his own. They, of course, did not, and in his hand he now held the perfect gift for his shadow.

Theo kept his newfound treasure tucked safely away in the breast pocket of his coat as he made a hasty stop by the storehouse. In his mind's eye, he envisioned what would have been a proper piece of jewelry—the iridescent pearl dangling daintily between her collarbones from an elegant chain. But despite his most thorough rummaging, he encountered no chains of any sort of metal, never mind the silver or gold he had been hoping for. He did, however, manage some strips of leather, a coil of wire, and a pair of needle-nose pliers. It would have to do.

What was supposed by him to have been an easy task turned out to be more arduous than he could have ever imagined. The pearl must first be wrapped in the thin wire if he was to string it onto one of the leather strips, but his fingers proved more cumbersome and clumsy than he ever knew. He wrapped and unwrapped the wire again and again, taking extra care to avoid scratching the pearl, and while he succeeded in leaving the pearl unscathed, the wire itself was a different story. He either clenched it so hard that the pliers left unseemly indentations on its surface, or his grip was so tentative that he couldn't coax it to bend in the way he wished.

When he looked up to see the stars twinkling through his window, he set the pearl and his frustrations aside, for he knew if he stayed awake too long his shadow would not come. With the candles blown out, Theo laid himself down in bed and closed his eyes.

Still Water

He fantasized about the necklace, thinking up different scenarios of what might happen when he could finally give it to her. Not a single one of these fantasies consisted of him leaving it on the doorstep the way a coward would. No, in his dreams he stood before her and handed it to her himself.

***

It was two weeks. Two weeks of evenings spent hunched over his little square table, fingers aching from the meticulously repetitive motion of wrapping and unwrapping wire, eyes heavy from the strain of working under flickering candlelight.

Two long weeks, but at last it was done.

He rejoiced, not for the simple sake of completing this wearisome deed—though that was certainly reason enough—but also for his unexpected delight at his own craftsmanship. By making it a point to remain patient and precise no matter his mental fatigue, he'd exacted a product that elicited from him a sense of pride rather than embarrassment.

Concealed within a pouch of linen stitched by Theo's own hand, he left the gift for her on the step. Though it pained him beyond belief to do so, he knew it wasn't a possibility to give it to her directly. Not yet.

His nerves were so fraught with anticipation that he knew sleep would be an impossibility on that night.

The initial offering of a cooked meal had been impersonal, something he would have passed off to a quotidian neighbor as a sign of general amicability. The necklace, on the other hand, represented something entirely different to him. It was a thing made with much more intimate intentions, meant to communicate a message beyond that which words might convey. It seemed to him that an entirely new realm of possibilities was opening up before him, like the many petals of a flower. This could be the beginning of something just as precious, just as delicate as the first breath of spring which thaws out the winter frost.

The sounds that accompanied her arrival came at their usual time. The muted crunch of snow, the quiet thump of the fish being set down, but it was the sound of her retreat that was yet unaccounted for. It was easy to imagine her standing just on the other side of the door, peering down at the pouch. Did her brow furrow with suspicion? Had she taken it into her hands, shifted it around in a half-hearted attempt to gauge its contents? Was it already suspended around her neck? Oh, how Theo longed to see such a sight.

But, alas, he could not. All he could do was lay there and hope that in a moment he would see her advance past his window once more. And so he waited, and through his cracked lids he was able to spy her figure as he had so many times before, only this time she did not skate so quickly by. Instead, she stood still as if to peer in through the glass. A plume of panic vaulted through Theo's chest. He prayed the moonlight had not reflected off of his eyes before he had the chance to close them.

With every muscle tensed into painstaking stillness, Theo waited for many long minutes to pass until he could be sure she had moved on. When he finally dared to peel open his eyes, he saw naught from beyond the window but gnarled tree branches and the blanket of darkness above them. He did not possess the courage to rise out of bed to check whether or not she had taken the necklace, for if she were still nearby it would reveal to her the deceptive nature of his slumber.

Theo wished for her to feel safe in the act of approaching his door, and he hoped that the gift had served as a token of encouragement to continue to do so. He liked to think it had.

Chapter Fourteen

Reciprocation—a concept Iris had yet to define for herself.

The tender, reeking meat could have passed for scraps left out for the birds, but this pouch and its perplexing contents were... well, *perplexing*.

Iris was nearly certain she'd grasped the concept though, the same way she'd come to an understanding of humans and their nests. She brought him fish, and so this was his attempt to present her with something in return. It was an offering, a cordial gesture. Almost like when she had left behind the corpses of the men who wished him harm on the sea-cage in return for her future meal.

Whether her human's offering would simplify or complicate things, she could not say. But her curiosity alone was enough to influence her to take it.

Iris leaned against a small crag near the edge of the canal, curling her tail beneath her in a comfortable seated position. She unlaced the pouch and emptied it into her palm. It was a pearl, but not the kind she'd ever seen. The longer she held it, the more she began to feel as if she were not holding a pearl at all, but something else entirely. Slowly, Iris brought her palm toward her face to inspect the shining orb. Beneath knitted brows she peered into it, trying to understand.

That was when she felt it, the initial pulse. Then another. And another.

The pearl seemed to throb from within, like an egg preparing to hatch. She watched and waited, but it did not outwardly move or crack the way an egg might. It did nothing but faintly thud against her skin, a steady beat that went on and on. Was it living? Breathing? What was this thing that her human had given to her? She felt for the strip of leather, hooking it onto her index finger and lifting it from her palm. The pearl dangled before her like a pendulum, producing a distorted reflection of her face on its smooth surface.

She wondered what she was meant to do with it. It could not be eaten, so what was its purpose? She did not know, but the way the pearl swayed from the strip of leather, it stirred up some vague memory, one she could not quite place. It had been during a hunt... No, during many hunts. Perhaps it was when—yes! That was it!

She had seen these sorts of trinkets before, and while she still did not know what they might signify, she was certain that they often hung from the throats that she sank her teeth into.

She pulled the cord over her head, feeling the dull thrum against her chest, and there it remained as she slithered back into the canal.

As the sky began shifting from plum to orange, Iris propelled herself through the channel until she broke back into the sea. She floated there for a moment, staring off into miles upon miles of cerulean. The weight of the pearl around her neck was impossible to ignore, and a part of her wanted to tear it off right then, to watch as it sank into the darkness below. But then she remembered her human and his many peculiar undertakings. Just like the fortifications of his nest, this unusual token must have been something he had toiled over, something he created with his own hands. The difference was that this creation had been not for himself, but for her. She did not know how that made her feel.

Iris missed the times when she felt nothing.

She rested there in the open waters for a long while. It could have been days or weeks, she did not know. Time slipped around her like the strong ocean currents, impossible to harness.

***

Idiot. Theo was a raging idiot. An utter fool to believe that leaving a gift for his shadow had been at all the sensible thing to do. He'd been too forthright, too brazen, and now she was gone. Days had passed since she last came in the night with her generous bestowals of fish, since he'd gazed upon her graceful shape through the window.

With a stony heart, Theo began to drown himself in his work. After all, it was for the best. No more frivolous pursuits to distract him, no more wasted time. The boat now took precedence over all else. Food and rest were postponed as long as physically possible, becoming a simple means to replenishing energy expended. Every moment between sunup and sundown was consumed by an obsessive drive to complete what he had originally set out to do. The sooner he could part with this haunted place, the better.

***

Despite her addled mind, Iris knew she should soon return to her lookout at the canal. Her human would likely be in want of a fresh supply of fish if she'd come to understand anything about the frequency with which he ate.

That evening she left a large ration to make up for lost time. On her way back to the water, she stopped to observe the pile of lumber that was his work. She could now see what it was he endeavored to make. It was a sea-cage, a miniature one; at least it would be when it was finished. Right now it was merely the bare bones.

She imagined all the energy he'd applied to it while she was away, the wood smoothly sanded and fitted together with such precise accuracy. It must have taken a great deal of his time and strength.

It was really quite a shame that he would never have a chance to put it to use.

***

Theo had assured himself that his focus was finally where it should be, that he was finally back on the proper path. It became his truth, and he believed in it with conviction. That was until he awoke one morning to find fish once more on his doorstep.

A quiet curse issued from his lips as he stooped to pick it up. He'd finally made peace with his circumstances and now she was back, bringing with her all the feelings he had endeavored to put behind him. Whether it was a cruel or kind turn of events, Theo could not decide. Nonetheless, she had come back. That had to mean something, did it not?

Theo glanced over at the skeleton of his boat, dusted with snow from the prior night's flurry. The sun that had begun to defrost the icy land those few weeks ago had returned to its resting place behind the clouds. The weather now grew colder and more bleak with each passing day, and the thought of a warm, fresh meal made Theo's mouth water and his stomach growl. He pivoted back into his cabin to cook the fish. Compared with the salted meat from the storehouse, its taste was divine.

Rather than crawling into bed as he usually did after blowing out the candles that evening, Theo settled himself on the floor just beside the door instead. It wasn't long before he heard the familiar sound of his shadow's approach. When he sensed that she was as close to the door as she would get, he whispered quickly, "Do not be afraid. Please, I beg of you. Do not leave."

He heard the utter stillness as she stiffened at the sound of his voice. Before she could take the opportunity to flee he again spoke. "I only wish to give my sincerest thanks for the kindness you've extended to me over these past weeks. And to apologize if I offended you with my gift."

Silence.

"Please, if you're still there, say something. Say anything. I merely wish to hear the sound of your voice so that I may have something tangible to associate with your generosity. You exist as a ghost in my mind. I fear I cannot bear it much longer," he breathed.

"A ghost?" she asked. Theo nearly wept at the sound of it, her voice was so clear, so pure.

"Yes, a ghost. A specter. A thing so evanescent, so transitory that it makes one question their own sanity."

"I do not understand," said the voice from the other side of the door.

"I simply mean..." He struggled to find words suitable to convey his sentiment. "I mean that I cannot believe you are here, speaking to me now. It almost seems a dream to me." A smile materialized on his lips as he spoke.

"Oh," was all she said.

"Would you mind if..." Theo began, placing a reluctant hand on the doorknob.

"No." The knob would not budge. She was holding it firmly from the opposite side to prevent its turning. Theo withdrew his hand as if from a scorching flame.

"I'm sorry," he said in earnest. "As I said before, I have no wish to offend. I simply thought—"

"I am not offended, not by your... gift, nor by your attempt to open this..."

"Door?" Theo finished for her.

"Yes, this door. But I do not want to be seen."

It took him a moment to gather his wits. She did not wish to be seen? Why ever not? What little he had gleaned of her through his window on all those nights had been beautiful, strikingly so. And the ringing of her voice further consecrated this belief in his mind. He felt sure it could not have been anything related to her appearance that rendered her so reluctant, which meant it must have been fear that compelled her to hide. She had not yet placed her trust in him, and for this he commended her. She knew nothing of him or his character. Save for the anonymous exchanging of goods on his doorstep, they were utter strangers to one another. It was wise of her to keep this barrier between them for the time being, to make him earn her faith.

"I understand and respect your wish completely. We can speak like this, through the door, if that is preferable to you. But please do tell me your name. Mine is Theo. Theo Carter." He nearly refrained from revealing his last name for fear that she might associate it with his father, but if he wished for her to open up to him then he owed her the same courtesy. She hesitated for a moment, probably weighing the risks of disclosing her own name.

"Iris," she said finally. "My name is Iris."

"Beautiful," Theo whispered. The sound of her retreat drew him from his daze. "Wait! Please, will you return tomorrow evening?"

The sound of her movement ceased. Theo awaited her response with bated breath.

"What for?" she asked him, a curious lilt in her voice.

He was unprepared to answer such a question. "So that we may speak to each other again—through the door, of course." he stuttered. "So that we may enjoy one another's company," he added with a bit more conviction, his every word coated with the sticky syrup of hope.

But she was already gone.

Chapter Fifteen

Iris had not moved all night. She was in the canal, eyes peeking over its edge in the direction of the land-cage.

"The-o," Iris said aloud, testing the syllables on her tongue. Her human's name was Theo. And according to Theo himself, he had enjoyed her company enough to ask her to return. Iris's inquisitive nature, alongside the innate flattery that stems from feeling desired by another, compelled her to grant Theo his wish.

But was it the wise thing to do?

During the hunts of her past, she'd only ever shared a few choice words with her prey, if any at all. Of course, this hunt was different from the others, but did that mean the rules changed? Did more time truly warrant more extensive speech?

There was no denying that speaking with Theo had been unlike speaking with those who came before him. He did not ask why she was doing this to him or beg to be spared. No, this was more so an invitation for... for what, exactly? For friendly conversation? She'd heard sailors speak to each other in such a manner from time to time. Perhaps that is what Theo wanted.

Friendly, however, was not quite within Iris's realm of understanding. She understood trickery and seduction. And though she was certainly no savant in the art of exchanging pleasantries, her talents just so happened to be diametrically opposed—making things quiet was her primary area of expertise. There were just so many ways to silence the pleas for life, for death, for anything that might put an end to physical suffering. But this—what Theo asked for now—she did not know if she could be capable of such things.

Floating there in the misty light of dawn, Iris asked herself if she wanted to find out.

***

"Hello?" she said to the door. It was a few hours past sunset and it had just begun to flurry. The thick, fluffy snowflakes looked like stars falling from the sky.

"Iris? Iris, hello," he said from the other side. Based on the sounds coming from within, he'd rushed over to the door from some deeper place within his land-cage. He sounded winded.

"You did not think I would return?" She spoke slowly, thinking carefully of each word before she said it.

"I must admit I did not," was his answer. "I thought I may have finally scared you away for good."

Iris did something strange then. She laughed. It produced an oddly pleasant feeling in her core.

"What?" Theo asked, and based on the way he enunciated the word, she wondered if he might match her laugh with one of his own.

"If I had stayed away, it would not have been for fear."

"Though I'm very glad to hear you're unafraid of me, your statement leads me to wonder at my own bearing. Do I truly appear so weak? So helpless?" His offense did not sound genuine, almost as if he found something about her words amusing.

"You might be strong. But I am stronger."

Theo shifted his weight as he considered the strangeness of her statement. He concluded that she must have been referring to her survival skills or something to that effect. It could very well be true that she was better equipped—both physically and mentally—to persist under their current conditions. "I see. I don't doubt that you and your people must be very strong to survive in a place such as this."

"I have no people."

"You mean to say you are completely on your own here?" He'd suspected as much, but hearing it aloud brought about an unexpected sense of disbelief.

"Yes. You are surprised by this?"

"Well… Yes. I suppose I am," he admitted.

They were both quiet for a moment.

"Have you been here very long?"

"Just as long as you."

He'd been subconsciously gravitating toward the door until his forehead touched its sanded planks.

"Was it a shipwreck?" he inquired, trying to recall if he'd happened upon any debris during his time on the beach. "The sea can be quite—"

"No. I chose to come here."

"You—you what? Why would you do such a thing?" The thought itself was astonishing to him.

"Does it matter? I am here now, and so are you."

"I simply wish to know more about you. That's all."

"But you do know me. I am Iris, the one who comes to speak to you through your door each night. There is no more to know."

"Of course there's more. Why, there is so much to—wait! Does that mean you plan to return again tomorrow?"

Iris straightened her spine, wondering what had given him that impression.

"What you just said—you called yourself 'the one who comes to speak to me through my door *each night*.' That means you will return, yes?"

An owl hooted from a nearby tree as Theo awaited her answer.

"Won't you?" he asked once more.

The owl grew quiet, as if he too were listening in anticipation.

"I have a…" she struggled to find the proper word, "a *ask*? I have a ask of my own first."

"A question? Yes, of course. You may ask me anything. Anything at all." His relief that she hadn't again disappeared into the night left him breathless.

"Have we just had what you would call a conversation?"

Theo laughed, expecting her to do the same, for her question must have been made in jest. But she did no such thing, remaining utterly silent. When he realized she had indeed been serious in her inquiry, he clamped his mouth shut at once.

"Why, yes," he quickly assured her. "We certainly have."

"And was it a good one?"

"Of course it was. It's been a long while since I've had such a nice conversation as that. And I mean that sincerely."

"Okay. Then I will return tomorrow." Iris had wished for her words to come across as composed and serious, but for some vexing reason she could not keep her lips from curling upwards, a minuscule movement that changed her tone completely. She was especially thankful for the door in that moment, lest he should see her rows of sharp teeth.

"I eagerly await your next arrival," Theo said, a wide grin on his own face. "But, Iris, before you go, can I offer you anything? A warm meal? Some tea, or a place here beside my hearth? I have some blankets I could spare if you would like to have them. Anything—anything at all? The chill out there is relentless."

"I am fine. I have all I need."

It felt wrong letting her go off into the cold night, but he knew he could not force her to stay.

"Of course. Goodnight then, Iris."

"Goodnight, Theo."

Theo and Iris had a sort of unspoken agreement from that point on. During the daylight hours they remained apart. This was the time when Theo focused on his boat, and Iris let him, seeing no harm in allowing him to keep himself occupied for the time being. She easily busied herself with catching him fish and covertly watching his work from the canal.

Come dusk, Theo would devour a quick meal before settling in on the floor beside the door to wait for Iris. Their conversations were like none he'd ever had before, and he quickly learned that she was different from anyone he'd ever known.

She vehemently disliked speaking of herself, instead wishing to hear about Theo and his life. Once comfortable, it seemed she had an endless stream of questions for him, some of them so absurd that he had to withhold his amusement for fear of making her feel embarrassed.

She once asked him what the garment he wore over his torso was called, and when he told her it was called a shirt she asked him why he wore it.

"Well, it is very cold here, is it not? We would freeze if we failed to properly cover ourselves."

"Yes, of course," she said quickly. She'd been growing more confident with her words, learning to emulate Theo's speech patterns at a rapid rate. "But if you were to live somewhere warmer than here, you would abandon this… shirt, no?"

Theo felt himself turning red despite the fact that he was alone within the walls of his cabin.

"Perhaps a man would cast aside his shirt upon certain occasions. Many do so while working in the heat."

"And what of women?"

"No, a woman would not abandon her shirt, not even if the weather was hot."

"Why not?"

"I suppose it is simply not the norm. Many would believe it indecent."

"What is this 'indecent' you speak of?"

It was in this way that their conversations grew longer and longer, lasting well into the late hours of night. And it was because of these conversations that Theo came to realize Iris may have experienced a rather unique upbringing. She was reluctant to reveal much about her personal history other than that she'd been alone for most of it. No family, no friends—nothing. While he felt sorry that she'd lived such an isolated life thus far, it was also what he credited her shrewd sense of self-sufficiency to. He reckoned her detachment from others is what had allowed her to remain so untamed and inquisitive—the parts of Iris that he'd grown particularly fond of.

One of the eccentricities that Theo was quite frankly less fond of was her rigidity when it came to the door. She remained on the outside while he remained within; it was a condition she was unwilling to budge on, no matter how he tried to change her mind. And so he contented himself with his imagination, envisioning her sleek black hair and smooth skin whenever they spoke.

One gusty evening, as they sat on their usual opposing sides, Theo had been doing just that. It was what prompted his next question.

"What color are your eyes?" he asked her.

"I don't know," was her response.

Would he ever be able to anticipate what strange thing Iris would say next? He certainly hoped not.

"You don't know? Have you never looked into a mirror?"

"No. Have you?" she asked earnestly.

"Of course I have," he said with a smile. "I have blue eyes and light brown hair. I've never been good about keeping it combed. My eyebrows are dark and thick—a bit too bold for my face, in my opinion. I've often been told they make me look angry, even when I'm not. A scar runs through the left one."

Iris listened carefully as Theo spoke, visualizing the familiar broad shoulders and the wild hair, the large hands that created and constructed with such ease.

"A scar?" she asked.

"Yes, a mark made by a past injury. One that doesn't fade away." She waited for him to say more—he usually had no qualms about elaborating—but this time he grew quiet enough to unsettle her.

"From what?"

He did not particularly wish to speak of the scar's origin, but found it difficult to deny Iris an answer.

"It comes from a time on my father's ship, a time when I was quite young—about eight or so, if I had to guess. The rum had raised his spirits that night, and so he asked me to join him in a game of cards. I could see clearly the glint of warning in Edris's eyes, but I—a mere boy grasping for his father's approval—agreed to let him teach me the rules of the game. Eager to impress, I eventually played a card in haste. As it was, the card should only have been played if I had none of the leading suit left in my hand. My mistake lent me a false victory, and my father grew suspicious. He demanded I show him my hand, after which he accused me of intentionally cheating. It was then that his suspicion turned to anger."

Theo's voice sounded far away, like he was retreating back into the memory.

"And he injured you?"

"He wanted me to stand up, I think. To 'face him like a man,' as he would have put it. So he tipped my chair and I fell. My head collided with the table on my way down. I don't think he intended…" His voice trailed off. "Anyway, I had Edris there to help me. He cleaned the wound and closed it up, and I was right as rain after that."

Iris's pupils dilated the way they would during a hunt. She yearned to spring on something, to tear it to shreds. She yearned to taste the blood of Benedict Carter.

"Where is he?"

"Who? Edris?"

"No, your father."

"My father is dead."

Disappointment coursed through Iris's veins like poison. Her fingers twitched with pent up wrath. That wrath clamored for release.

"Theo, I am going to leave now."

"Wait, Iris. Why—"

"Goodnight."

Her body lanced through the thrashing waves. It would seem that the ocean was angry too on this night. She and the sea became one, a raging tempest that would lay waste to any who dared to sail through their waters.

Iris let the storm feed her fury, and she gave herself over to the ocean's ferocious swells until they both had no fight left to give.

CHAPTER SIXTEEN

There'd been no fresh snowfall for days, but the blanket of mid-January snow that already coated the ground had nearly frozen solid. The weather had otherwise remained fair, and as long as he could avoid slipping on the ice beneath his feet, Theo had been able to get in a good six or seven hours of work per day. The supporting frame of the boat's hull was now fastened to the keel, and plans of erecting a mast for the eventual rigging of a sail were in the works.

Unfortunately for Theo, weather is but a volatile and ever-changing thing, and clement conditions cannot persist forever. The day on which he'd been set to raise the mast, chunks of ice began raining down from the sky. All he could do was hope that his hard work would not be smashed to bits by the fist-sized balls of hail.

Being confined within the cabin to wait out the storm left Theo feeling antsy, and he spent most of the long hours fretting over Iris. The day had nearly passed, and still he was utterly confounded by her abrupt departure the night before. He rehashed their conversation again and again, wondering what it was he could have said to upset her so. If she had told him of his blunder rather than fleeing, then perhaps they could have talked things through and she could have taken shelter from the storm within the cabin. Theo knew not where she went when she wasn't on the opposite side of his door, but he prayed that she had made it somewhere safe before the sudden onset of this squall.

Eventually the weather let up. It was too dark to assess any damages sustained to the boat, and so he was again left with a stint of empty time. He filled it by rifling through the cabin's various chests and drawers until he found the object he sought.

Theo was already sitting beside the door with it in hand when he heard her drawing near.

"Iris," he said. "How did you fare through the storm? Well, I hope."

"I'll remind you once more that you needn't worry about me. I am fine. And you, Theo? Did your shelter fare well?"

He glanced up at the roof. "As far as I can tell all still seems to be standing. I only hope I will be able to say the same for the boat come tomorrow."

"The boat?" Iris asked. Theo did not know that Iris had yet to learn the word that mankind bestowed upon their "sea-cages" so long ago, and so her question was interpreted by him as a sign of disapproval.

"Yes," he began, unsure of how the topic should be broached. "I plan to take it out on the water eventually. Have a sail around so that I might get my bearings."

It was not a lie that he'd spoken. He had true and honest intent to do just as he said; it was the minor detail of his subsequent departure that he withheld. What good would that kind of talk do either of them now, anyhow? The time was still so far off, and he would bring it up to her in due time. Perhaps she would even agree to accompany him by then.

"Anyway, I was thinking about what we spoke of last night, and I have something I would like you to see," Theo continued, eager to steer their thoughts away from the boat.

Iris said nothing. The pearl thumped against her sternum.

"I will have to open the door to give it to you though," Theo said, sounding unsure.

Iris was hesitant with her response. She wanted to see what it was he spoke of, but also worried he might see her.

"You may open the door," she said finally. "But you must refrain from looking this way or I will leave and never again return."

"I would never go against your wishes, Iris. You must know this by now," he assured her.

She was quiet.

"May I open it now, then? Without alarming you?" his voice was almost a whisper. Iris could not help but smile at his apparent shyness.

"Yes," she said.

Theo exercised caution, opening the door with a slow-moving mindfulness. Iris watched, every fiber of her being taut, as the glowing yellow light escaped from within to illuminate the outline of Theo's hand. The first thing she noticed were the veins, the way they pushed up against his skin just enough to cast the most intriguing shadows over its dorsal side. Then his knuckles, callused and hard, and the little blond hairs protruding from the tops of his fingers. She had the strangest desire to discover if those hairs could truly be as soft as they appeared, to lean in close enough to count them all, one by one, and catalog the number in her mind. There was a line of dirt beneath each of his fingernails, the telltale mark of a terrestrial being, one who lives on and from the soil.

Iris realized that she liked that about him, about humans in general. They were built to carry with them that which makes them what they are, and to carry it so that any who take the time to look will see it, *know* it.

And what did Iris carry of herself? She had no nails beneath which to accumulate dirt or sand, and her skin could not be kissed by the sun, nor could she bear the scars of her past feats. What proof was there that she existed at all?

In Theo's hand was what appeared to be a small pane of glass affixed to a silver handle. He gingerly set it down on the step and then closed the door. Iris looked at it, reluctant to move.

"What is it?"

"Pick it up and see," was all he said.

She acquiesced to his request, taking the cool metal in her hand. When she lifted it, she was met by her own reflection. Iris had never before seen herself more clearly than in this moment. The vacantness of her features startled her, and she thrust the mirror from her face and down into her lap where she would not have to look at it.

"Well?" Theo asked, and she lurched at the sound of his voice. She looked at the door, her expression cross. "Well what?"

"What color are they? Your eyes?"

Iris's icy demeanor melted some, and she took a deep breath so as to steel herself for one last look, if only to answer Theo's question.

"Black," she said after a moment. Black, hollow, catatonic. She looked and looked and found a great nothing within them.

Chapter Seventeen

A human's eyes were like windows; within them one might find a great many things. Fear, lust, pain, joy. Iris had looked into many of these windows and descried the endless worlds which they held. But never had she looked upon a pair of eyes so devoid of anything as her own.

Perhaps through her conversations with Theo, she could learn how to fill that emptiness.

That night Theo seemed quieter than usual. His scent gave off no sign of sickness or injury, so Iris struggled to understand what could be the matter.

"What ails you?" she finally asked.

"What do you mean?" His tone betrayed that he was unsurprised by her question.

"You've scarcely spoken a word this evening. Would you prefer to be alone?"

"No, of course not. I apologize for my low spirits. I've been dwelling too much in my thoughts."

"Your thoughts—they are bad ones?"

"Yes, I'm afraid so."

Iris was quiet for a moment, thinking. "Tell me of them. I wish to know."

Theo exhaled loudly. "I don't know that I should."

"Tell me," she implored him. "Please," she added, remembering the word Theo used anytime she refused him something.

"I worry you'll misunderstand my feelings. I'm unsure of my ability to convey them properly."

The pain in his voice made Iris's pupils dilate. Her vision grew sharp enough to discern a fox sniffing through the brush some eighty feet away. She tried to calm herself, to focus on Theo's words so that she would not have to resort to abruptly excusing herself like the last time.

"How could I misunderstand if you tell it to me plainly?"

He could not refuse her, no matter how much he may have wished to. "Fine then. It may not come out as plainly as you might think, but I will begin with the simple part—I am deeply unhappy," he began. "That is easy enough to understand, I think. The difficult part of it is that I am also the happiest I've ever been."

Iris cocked her head. "And how can that be?"

Theo laughed sullenly. "I told you it wasn't so simple. You see… It wasn't long ago that I'd come to the conclusion that I had nothing left to live for; it's a feeling I still struggle with, even now. But at the same time, it's impossible to deny that your presence has changed things for me. Because of you I feel… I feel hope. You are a light in my darkest hour, guiding me from the demons that haunt me."

Iris was familiar with the negative connotation that came with that word—"demons." In fact, it had been an adjective used to describe her more than a few times. She thought of Theo's eyes—his human eyes, flooded with all his conflicted human emotions—being plagued by darkness. Could she really be this light that he spoke of?

"I would like to help you, Theo. If I can help you escape these demons, I will."

Iris placed her hand on the door, feeling its lifeless grains against her palm. She could hear Theo's choked breath coming from the other side, heard him work to regain control before he dared to speak again.

"There was one person in this entire world who's ever truly needed me, and I've failed her miserably. Clara, my sister, has disappeared, vanished—and it was under my care that it happened. The guilt lives inside me now, always. Every moment of every day I am tortured by it, and because of that I do not know that I will ever be able to truly *feel* the happiness you've brought me. Only once I find her will my soul finally be able to rest."

"Clara?" Iris asked, the name ringing a bell in her mind. Then it came to her—small fingers clenching mangled purple flowers, a smile of innocence, crinkling storm cloud eyes, so much like Theo's but without all the hurt. Iris felt it in the pit of her stomach, the twisting pang of a thing called regret.

"Oh Theo, I am sorry. I am so very sorry," she said, though he could not have understood the true meaning behind her words.

"Tell me, Iris. Do you think me a fool for believing she's somewhere out there still? And that I might find her if she is?"

"You are no fool. She... She's out there somewhere. She must be." She said it to assuage his pain, though the words tasted like dirt on her tongue now that she knew what she knew. Theo may not have had any young of his own, but he'd had a sibling. His familiar tantalizing scent, the small coat he carried with him when he plunged from the ship—it all made sense now.

"Thank you. For being here with me. For listening to my incoherent ramblings."

"Do not thank me. Please, do not thank me."

"Of course I should thank you. God only knows where I'd be if he hadn't sent you to me."

"God?" Iris asked, alarmed. She'd heard the name before. Men often begged the one called God to save them from her hunger, though he'd never answered their calls. Had he truly spoken to Theo? How much did he know of her plans, of what she had done?

"You've never heard of God?" Within Theo's question there was no judgment or even surprise, merely an honest desire to know her answer.

She feigned ignorance. "No. Who is he? Where might one find him?" Perhaps she could kill God and be rid of him before he could tell Theo anything more.

"Hmm..." Theo struggled to put the concept into words. He scarcely knew his own feelings when it came to such matters, so providing Iris with a cogent explanation proved most challenging. "Many believe God is an all-powerful being, one who decides our fate. That those who follow his tenets and praise his name will be rewarded with eternal life and any who turn their back on him will be damned to everlasting hell."

Iris laughed. Outright laughed. And despite Theo's initial dark mood, her mirth encouraged him to crack a smile.

"What is so funny about that?" he asked.

"It just sounds so very... strange. So he is not here? He is not a man we could go speak to if we wished?"

"That depends on who you ask."

"I am asking you. Do you believe in these things?"

"I don't know. I think..." he grew quiet. "I think God is hope. Yes, that is what I believe." He nodded to himself, suddenly very sure of it.

Any humor that the absurdity of "God" had evinced within Iris was drained away just as quickly as it had come, leaving behind a sickly feeling in its wake.

***

Priorities became moving parts for Theo, endlessly shifting this way and that.

Sometimes, when the morning light grazed the lids of his eyes, he would wake eager to set his hands on the boat, determined to make as much ground as possible before sunset. But more and more often he awoke inspired to take on some new impromptu project, almost always unrelated to his work. Things such as carving a spear for Iris to fish with or sprucing up the cabin doorstep with moss-filled cushions gradually began to take more precedence. These were the days on which he remembered what it was to feel happiness, to forget his many cares. Of course it was just a facade; the rose colored curtain came crashing down and guilt reared its ugly head anytime the neglected boat came into his line of sight.

Still Water

It seemed to Theo that he was stuck in the middle of two separate worlds, each pulling him in opposite directions. He daydreamed of splitting himself in two, sending one half to rescue Clara and allowing the other half to remain where he was with Iris. He soon became obsessed with trying to divide his time equally between duty and pleasure, and found that this somehow made things worse. Quantifying the amount of minutes, hours, and days he'd deprived from his search for his sister made him feel wicked to the point that his every act seemed perverse. Even the things he knew he *should* be doing, such as attempting to map out a route to the Horned Isle, now felt wrong.

Still, no matter how tormented he became, he tried to keep his thoughts of it to himself. Though they weighed heavily on his heart, he had no wish to afflict Iris any further than he already had with his many woes.

He wished for Iris's nightly visits to remain lighthearted, a repose from reality, and so he had recently taken to reciting his favorite childhood stories to her instead. He was delighted to learn that she was unfamiliar with the whole lot of them, and he took great pleasure in untucking them from his memory one by one.

He told the stories to the door, through which he could sense Iris's rapt attention as he led her through world after world of whimsy and magic. And though he oftentimes worried she might find his next story dull or silly, her earnest questions always assured him otherwise.

"Who were the children of this Fairy God Mother?"

"Why would a giant care so much for gold?"

"What could possibly be ugly about a duckling?"

Like Theo, Iris seemed to have an innate love for works of the imagination. So when he stumbled upon a book complete with crumbly, mildewed pages while nosing through a nearby cabin for extra supplies, he greedily took it into his possession. It had been so long—*too* long—since he'd held such a treasure in his hands.

One of the first things Edris had ever taught Theo was to look for books during their campaigns, promising that their pages carried more wealth than any amount of gold could ever afford them. Theo recalled his father's complaints regarding the weight of the many tomes they'd acquired over the years, often threatening to throw them all overboard so that they might sail faster. But for reasons unbeknownst to Theo, Carter never made good on his word.

Anyway, the books were gone now, every last one of them. Sunken in some indiscriminate part of the ocean. Theo at least took some comfort in the thought that wherever Edris had wound up, perhaps his collection of stories had followed him there.

He had been thinking of Edris more frequently as of late, calling forth his memory in his times of need. Edris had been wise and moderate, whereas his father had been rash and barbaric, and to Benedict Carter's overall disdain, his son had taken a preference to learning how to properly read, write, and speak over knowing how and when one should keelhaul a member of his crew.

Like with the books, Carter routinely threatened to be rid of Edris and his "learned ways" as well. But again, he never followed through. The older Theo got, the more he puzzled over that.

There were vague memories that sometimes floated around Theo's head, memories which he could not be certain were real or imagined. It was a recollection of voices coming from deep within his father's quarters. Benedict and Edris, speaking of things that only educated men spoke of—literature, philosophy, politics, all muffled behind closed doors. For the entirety of his adult life Theo had been left to wonder if his father hadn't been as brutish as he made himself out to be. If, perhaps, this strange, secret companionship between two men had been the reason why Edris hadn't been put to death the moment he began teaching Theo his letters. If it could have been the reason he learned his letters at all.

As Theo opened his most recent acquisition to see what kind of stories its pages might tell, he found that it held no tales at all, but rather pages upon pages of personal logs. It mattered not to Theo, though. He was simply excited to have something new to share with Iris.

That evening, there on the splintered floor of his cabin, he orated the words on the pages to her. It began as the mundane recounting of sowing seeds and hunting alongside the other village men, logs of supplies and records of the weather. But the prosaic accounts quickly became something indisputably bizarre and potentially ominous.

"*'A thing of most terrible beauty, she is,'*" Theo read aloud at one point. "*'Men and women alike drive themselves mad to appease her, sacrificing their sisters and brothers, husbands and wives, daughters and sons to her endless hunger in the hopes that they might be repaid with even a fleeting moments' glance. There is a mysticism about her, a witchiness that will take one's soul and turn it to dust. She will be revered and forsaken for it. And this island will be damned for it. I will be damned for it, for I fear it is love I feel for her after all. Even worse, I fear she might love me in return.'*"

"Why've you stopped?" Iris asked.

"My eyes are tired," he said as an excuse. "These entries—they've grown rather strange, have they not?"

"I suppose so."

"Do they scare you?"

Iris looked up at a vaporous night sky. "No. Do they scare you, Theo?"

"They… unsettle me. I find the way that he speaks of his lover—almost as if she were a monster—to be quite unnerving."

The corners of Iris's mouth fell. "You think her a monster?"

"Don't you?"

"I don't know. I haven't yet decided."

After absorbing his fair share of silence, Theo asked, "What are you thinking of now?"

"I am thinking that you are afraid of the unknown, though that is not to say your fear is misplaced. And what of you and your thoughts?"

"I'm thinking that this is a peculiar place. This logbook, that—that *statue*. Everything is so very strange."

"Statue?"

"Yes, the one right outside there. You've seen it, haven't you? It's a woman, but with a fish's—"

"I believe I've seen it," Iris said shortly.

"It all makes for a rather disquieting atmosphere, don't you think? I'm led to wonder if those who lived here truly believed in this nonsense."

"I cannot say."

The icy reticence in Iris's voice gave Theo the impression that perhaps she truly was frightened and simply did not wish to say so. He decided he would store the logbook away from now on and speak of these matters no more.

Chapter Eighteen

Iris had always known that it was she who plagued mankind's most bedeviled dreams, so why did hearing it come from Theo's lips trouble her so?

The last of the day's light was ebbing, turning the somber, twisting branches above into misty shadows. She stared at those shadows without really seeing them, for her mind was preoccupied with thoughts of the human who had somehow become her greatest affliction. He would soon take his usual place behind the door in anticipation of her arrival, and while she was aware that her absence would likely cause him some form of emotional distress, it didn't change the fact that she was unsure if she wanted to speak to him.

She may have eventually left the comforts of the water and reluctantly made her way to Theo's cabin had it not been for the words that reverberated through her mind.

"You think her a monster?"

"Don't you?"

He'd said it so plainly, as if she'd asked him if he thought the sun would rise come morning.

The more she thought of it, the worse it stung, until finally her melancholic mood dictated she spend her night with her tail nestled deep in the silt on the canal floor, where she could at least ensure her own solitude.

There Iris remained, wrapped within the stream's cold and indifferent caress, looking out toward a liquid moon.

Never in all of Iris's obscure number of years had she encountered more questions than she had in these past weeks. She was losing sight of herself, of her place amongst living things. The natural world dictated that one must eat or be eaten, and Iris found it difficult to believe in exceptions to that rule. She was a mortal creature of the earth, and therefore she must consume other mortal creatures in order to go on living. The shark feels no moral qualms about eating the seal, and why should it? If it reserves the ability to do so then it must, lest it forfeit its own life. That was the way of things.

Eat or be eaten.
Eat or be eaten.
Eat or be eaten.

An echoed prayer, the unflinching wisdom of the collective many who preceded Iris's comparatively small existence.

Her instincts had never led her astray before. If she could just trust in those instincts rather than muddle her mind with these ceaseless questions, then perhaps things could return to the way they had once been.

Just as she managed to lull herself into her waking dreams, she was alerted by a voice—Theo's voice—ringing clearly through the water and into her ears.

"Iris?" The sound of his footsteps crunching over snow. "Iris? Are you there?"

He whispered toward the woods in a voice that was far too loud for his own good. Anything that might lurk within a one-mile radius was bound to have heard him, and those who hadn't most certainly sensed the intoxicating heat of his blood curling through the frosted air.

It was scarcely a moment later that Iris felt Theo's stillness. Seconds passed in tautly drawn silence, then came the distinct sound of rustling branches, of something moving through the brush. She imagined Theo trying to furtively take stock of his surroundings, knowing his dull human eyes would likely be unable to pinpoint much of anything in the dark anyhow.

Iris strained to see from the edge of the canal, where a great chunk of granite obstructed her view. She wished for the source of the noise to be a rabbit or a mouse, a thing harmless and soft, but this fantasy of hers was short lived.

Iris heard the first low growl before Theo did. By the time they grew close enough for his ears to detect it, there remained no outlet for his escape. Too many yellow eyes appeared in the shadows, all tracking him with the same impatient hunger. He took one cautious step backward and was rewarded with a bloodthirsty snarl, a warning to remain where he stood. Then the eyes began to shift about, moving to surround Theo so as to detect even the slightest twitch of a muscle. Slowly, the circle began to close in.

The scent of the beasts encircling Theo was familiar to Iris, very much like the stench of the shell-less crab she had killed in the months prior. That creature had been irritating, yes, but in a merely bothersome way, like a pest that needed shooing. The difference here was a matter of hunger—the pestering one had been nowhere near as starved as those who stood before her human now, and hunger always had a way of making things so much more lethal.

Iris listened to the standoff from the shoreline, her next act not yet decided. The hunters snarled and growled and snapped their jaws, but none had yet amassed the courage to go in for the kill. She sensed that at any moment one of them would break the taut thread of tension, and then Theo would be lost for good.

Iris could have risen from the canal to wreak havoc on these wretched beasts—it would have been a most simple errand, one that might have even brought her a sense of gratification—but it was not the task itself that had aroused her hesitation. It was the thought of revealing herself, the conscious awareness that her presence would inspire just as much—or perhaps *more*—fear within Theo as the fiends that endangered him now.

He would be unable to draw a distinction between savior and assailant because, to him, they were one and the same; all of them monsters. And so Iris was left with two impossible choices—she could save Theo's life and forfeit the singular connection she'd ever made with another living being, or she could refrain from helping him and leave their fellowship unblemished.

She made her choice calmly, deciding she would not allow the scavengers to feast upon his remains when it was over.

***

Theo remained unmoving as he assessed the situation. There were five wolves surrounding him, fangs bared and eager to draw blood. To his left was the canal, and to his right were the woods. Behind him lay the eastern border of the settlement, putting the safety of his cabin somewhere close to a mile west of where he now stood. Could he make it there before five adult wolves could? Unlikely. Did he have any other choice? Unfortunately not.

Knowing these would very likely be his final waking moments, he sent out a silent prayer that the presence of these wolves was unrelated to Iris's absence that evening. He also wished he could have had the chance to look into her eyes, to feel the warmth of her touch at least once before he died. But most of all he was grateful that their paths had crossed at all, even if it was for so brief a time.

He took comfort in the thought that, although his soul may never truly rest, it had at least been afforded the privilege of finding Iris.

Theo expelled one last deep breath from his lungs, and in a swift motion he turned and ran, using the element of surprise to burst through the circle of teeth. He ran as his legs had never ran before, feet striking the ground in a succession of quick, hard thumps. His muscles burned and his vision blurred around the edges as he tried with all his might to stay one step ahead of his pursuers. He could hear clearly the sound of their pants, the paws thrusting their lithe bodies over snow, root, and rubble. He swore he even felt their hot breath on his heels at times, but he kept on running, knowing if he faltered even a fraction of a step they would be upon him.

His cabin was not yet in sight, but one of the storehouses was. If he could just make it past the threshold and fasten the door behind him, he might just live to see tomorrow after all. If it hadn't been for one haplessly loose stone which got caught on the toe of his boot, he may have actually made it there.

Toppling to the ground, Theo curled into a ball and covered his head with both arms in an instinctual effort to shield himself from the oncoming attack. He waited for what felt like an eternity for teeth to tear into flesh, but it never came. Only once he heard a whimper did he finally have the courage to look up, and what he saw he struggled to comprehend.

Five gray wolves, lips curled to bare their starved smiles, bodies crouched close to the ground, ears flattened to their skulls in submission. Theo could not believe his eyes as he beheld these apex predators pacing and whining in what was impossible to mistake for anything but *fear*. He then realized it was not himself that solicited such meekness from the wolves, but whatever it was that stood behind him. Scrambling into an upright position, he turned and saw it—the Mourner. He could not possibly begin to fathom why, but this pack of vicious canines had been cowed by the effigy of a fish-tailed woman.

One by one the wolves turned and pranced off, tails between their legs, leaving Theo unharmed beneath the watchful eye of his inanimate protector.

CHAPTER NINETEEN

Iris.

That was Theo's one and only thought.

Had she, like himself, managed to escape the maw of those vile menaces in one piece? Or had some unthinkable atrocity befallen her?

He would have liked to begin combing through the sporadic thickets of wood at once, but he knew that wolves were often crepuscular, most active during the hours of dawn and dusk. If he had any sense at all he would wait well into mid-morning if he wished to avoid a second unfortunate encounter with the pack.

But how unbearable those hours were. For Theo to remain within the asylum of his cabin, to stare through the windows with dread in his heart, the adagio of crickets his only means of measuring the night's slow tempo, and to do so all without knowing if Iris still breathed life into her lungs.

Once he'd given the sun ample time to settle in for the day, he set out to find her, though he knew not where he should begin. Iris had always been so disinclined to share anything of herself that he'd never learned where it was she lived. It was a detail he often wondered over, but his fear of prying into her life beyond his doorstep had prevented him from ever directly asking. It had been but an innocent effort to avoid driving her away, but Theo could now see how great his folly had truly been. Avoiding the conversation had been the easy way out; the more difficult path would have been well worth the knowledge that she hadn't been eaten alive by wolves.

As he walked, keen eyes sifting past trees, brush, and sharp stones, he cursed himself for all the times he'd resorted to taking the easy way out—obeying his father's orders to remain in the Barren

Crest, falling into such complacency there, subjecting Clara to a bleak and lonely existence. How could he ever forgive himself for it? All those years spent skinning beavers so he could "buy their way out" had merely been a way of avoiding the truth. He'd known that the Barren Crest was no place for a child to grow, knew there were more expedient ways of leaving, if only he had looked harder for them. After years of living under his father's thumb, he had simply been too afraid to take control. And that was a mistake he'd paid dearly for.

His eyes grew misty as he steered himself through mazes of crooked trees.

"Iris!" he called, throat hoarse and voice cracking with desperation. The idea that he'd lost her too was unfathomable. He did not think he could bear it. "*Iris!*"

Theo walked through the dim of twilight, then into the break of night. After so many hours, there finally came a point when his vocal chords had grown so very raw, his legs so very weak that he could go no further.

He knew not where his feet had carried him, nor was he able to discern the route back to the settlement, but his aching muscles gave him no choice but to remain idle anyhow, at least for a few moments. Perhaps a short stint of rest would restore him so that he might piece together the way from which he came.

A nearby pile of dead leaves suddenly looked more inviting than any feathered pillow he'd ever seen. He laid his head upon it, hoping to regain even a morsel of his strength. Then he closed his eyes and whistled, and in his dreams Clara and Edris heard his call.

***

When Iris found him, he was curled up in the snow, a few soggy leaves tangled in the mess of his hair. She had heard his calls of despair, heard his pathetically sputtering excuse of a whistle, but she hadn't sacrificed so much to keep herself hidden all this time just to flaunt her tail any time he decided to make a foolish foray into the woods. So she had kept close behind him, following the trail of his scent until he finally wore himself out.

The sight of him lying there on the ground was rather demoralizing. His entire existence was so very fragile, so breakable, like the papery wings of a moth. She realized then that she must accept what was, for her, a difficult truth—there were a great many things beyond herself that could tear those wings of life from his soft thorax. Wolves, disease, storms, fevers, droughts—even *himself*. He could so easily be stolen away.

She stooped down, lifting him with ease. His bare cheek brushed against her arm, and she was reminded of how soft his skin was, how warm. She held to her bosom a blooming bouquet of his essence, ripe and sharp, enriching her olfactory senses. His scent was intoxicating, and she breathed it in the way she would her final breath of life.

Animalistic instincts coaxed Iris to gather him into her, to bury her face in the crook of his neck. Here, his jugular fluttered with life. So thin was the skin upon which she grazed her teeth. All it would take was one small nick to split the buttery flesh, to release the simmering copper that coursed beneath it. She could almost taste it—the precious blood that was to belong to her and her alone. She could take it now, drink in every last drop just to ensure that the opportunistic wolves would never see another chance to take what was hers.

Theo shifted so that his head lolled back a bit more, as if adjusting himself for her convenience. A small groan emitted from his throat, a sound that startled Iris so that she withdrew. She struggled to understand the affection she felt for him in that moment, for she could not decide if it was simply hunger or something else entirely that had driven all these strange thoughts into her mind.

Before her emotions could become anymore confused, she slithered back in the direction of his cabin, where she laid him beneath the covers of his bed. She was almost certain from hearing his footsteps so often that he usually didn't wear his boots inside, so she took a moment to figure out the laces and pulled them from his feet.

Setting them down at his bedside, Iris decided to have a look around before leaving. For all the time she'd spent gazing at the cabin's exterior, she'd never seen what it was like within.

Scattered across the table were some sketches of boats and maps, and on the counter were jars of herbs and a jug of water from the well. He kept a small stack of firewood beside the hearth and there was a single plate and cup set beside the window to dry out after washing.

She wished to touch every item Theo owned, to understand why he had them, what their purposes were. Then she wanted to watch as he used them to do whatever odd little things he did.

She wanted to watch him live.

But she left it all untouched, her hand only coming into contact with the door as she closed it behind her.

***

Theo was quite disoriented to have woken in his own warm bed and not one made of sticks and leaves. He could not pretend to know how he'd been spirited back to the cabin, but he certainly suspected that Iris and her strange ways had been in some way responsible.

If this were true though, it begged the question as to *how* she had gotten him there. He'd seen her silhouette many times through his window, and she had always appeared to be an average sized woman. Theo, on the other hand, carried the additional weight that comes with the height and lean muscle of the average working man. So unless Iris was uncommonly strong for one of her stature, he did not think it possible for her to have supported his mass for any substantial distance. Perhaps she was in possession of a wagon or cart of some sort. If she could have managed to hoist him into it, then this certainly could have been a sound explanation as to how he'd been transported.

Why, though? Why go to the trouble of lugging him over the rocky, snow covered hills back to his cabin? Why remove his boots and tuck him into bed when she could not even bother to answer him when he called?

Hope is a mysterious and potent thing, and it was that which drove Theo to wait near the door that night, even when his sense of reason told him he was a downright fool to think she might come. He was genuinely surprised when her voice came from the other side.

"Theo?"

"Iris," he breathed. "Yes, I'm here." He scrambled to his feet and, without thinking, seized hold of the door knob. It was held fast from the other side.

"No," she said, an edge to her voice. "If you open this door, I will leave. I mean it, Theo."

He jumped back as if bitten. "Forgive me. I had forgotten myself in my excitement. But, Iris, you must tell me, are you well?"

"Of course I am well," she said incredulously.

"But it's been two nights since you vanished. And then the—the *wolves* and... Well, I suppose what I'm trying to say is I've grown exceedingly worried."

"I wish you hadn't." Her tone was clipped and short. "I did not vanish, I simply did not come. And I am here now to inform you that all your worries have been gravely misdirected. Why is it that you have no consideration for your own well-being? Is it truly still your desire to die? I thought you'd moved past all that ridiculousness."

Theo almost could not believe his ears. Iris was angry with him. It was surprisingly exhilarating.

"So it *was* you."

"What?" she snapped.

"It was you who brought me back last night. But how did you do it?" The wonder in his voice incensed her further.

"That is neither here nor there. Focus now. You must develop a sense of self-preservation. I am able to save myself, but you must understand, Theo. I cannot save you."

Theo scoffed. "I am not in need of your saving. I would have been perfectly fine to spend a night in the woods. In fact, it may have even done me some—"

"No. You are still not understanding," she barked. "You were right to think this a strange place. It *is* a strange place, a *dangerous* place. And you were most certainly right in your fear of monsters."

"Iris, what in God's name are you on about?"

"Just listen to me, will you? Your God cannot save you and neither can I. Those wolves—they would have made a meal of you if it hadn't been for sheer luck. You were an absolute fool to go strolling so near to the woods in the middle of the night, and worse, with no means of defending yourself. What were you thinking?"

Theo's brow knit in frustration. Where was all this coming from? "I was looking for *you*."

"Don't."

"Iris—"

"Do not look for me. I have no wish to be found."

"And why not? Why all this secrecy? All this mistrust? Do you have no faith in me at all? In my intentions?"

"That is not what this is about. It's nothing to do with trust."

"What, then? Why can we not look each other in the eye when we speak?" Theo's blood was rushing with adrenaline, with indignation.

"Because we cannot!" Iris exclaimed.

"Because we cannot? *That* is your explanation—because we cannot? Why? For God's sake, Iris, just tell me already!"

"Because you would not like what you saw," she said suddenly, her voice going soft.

"You couldn't be more wrong about that, Iris. I would never—"

"I know I am not wrong. You must finish your boat and leave this place." She'd managed to find her resolve, firm and unyielding. They were both quiet as her words sunk in.

"If you've come to know me at all, you would think better of me than that," Theo finally said.

Iris recoiled from the evident injury in his voice. The conversation could not endure much more, that was clear, and she soon left in a rather sullen state.

She disliked this feeling—feeling as though she'd disappointed Theo. He had always held her in such high regard, and it now seemed as if she failed him in some way. But how? She'd only been trying to help.

Naturally, as any able-bodied creature strives to mitigate their various discomforts, Iris wished to remedy this pestilent blister which bit somewhere deep within her breast, but she knew not how. So she retired back to the water to think.

Chapter Twenty

Iris was used to stillness, used to long stints of meditation. But this? This raging turmoil that writhed so tirelessly within her? She feared she'd never grow accustomed to it.

Did she truly wish for Theo to leave? After all, that was what she had told him. But now, alone once more in the water, her only wish was to be near him again.

Could that truly be her desire—to be close to him, to hear the music of his voice, to feel his flesh against hers? Or did she really wish to possess him, taste him, devour him whole before anyone else could?

Was it possible to want both?

***

"I've thought things over since we last spoke," Iris said to Theo the following night. "And I believe seeing each other can be arranged."

"So we can open the door at last?" he asked gladly.

"No." She tried to keep her voice gentle as she said it. "We may see each other soon, but I have certain conditions that must first be agreed upon."

"Anything. Name these conditions you speak of."

***

Iris had never seen a compass, nor was she familiar with the cardinal directions. These inane words—north, south, east, and west—were intuitive feelings to one such as herself, already built in at her inception.

So when she was faced with the task of delineating the way to the caverns to Theo, she did it the best way she knew how—with the use of hyper-specific landmarks.

"You will come upon a tree that's been cleaved in half by a lightning bolt. When you see it, you will continue on until you reach the double-crested boulder. Then you must follow the more narrow path through..."

Eventually Theo had to explain that this method would never work.

"The sun rises in the east and sets in the west. My cabin is facing northward, and behind it is south," he began. "Can you tell me in which of these directions I must go?"

She took in this data, attempting to translate her markers into something Theo would understand.

"You will follow the sun westward through the woods. When you emerge, you will find yourself at the sea. From there the cliffs will be... north? Yes, north. Walk beside the sea until you come to them. Then light your torch and select an entrance into the caves."

"An entrance? There will be more than one?"

"Yes, but it won't matter which you choose. Inside, it's all connected. Just follow the sound of the water and from there I will come to you."

Theo shifted, apprehension tamping down his excitement.

"Are you sure you have no wish of traveling together? I would worry far less if we did."

"It would defeat my purpose," Iris said. "We travel separately. Worry not, for there's no reason to fret as long as you are able to deliver yourself to the caverns in one piece. Will you be able to manage that, Theo?"

Theo could manage slaying a dragon if it meant seeing Iris at last. "Of course."

***

STILL WATER

Iris's terms were indeed peculiar, but could Theo truly claim to have expected anything less? She was a skittish creature, overly cautious; this he knew well enough. So rather than question why he must trek through endless miles of tree and snow so that he might finally see her, he chose to focus instead on the fact that she had agreed to allow him to see her at all. In the end, he had managed to work himself into a very festive mood, one that entreated him to hum all the while he made his preparations for the trip.

The arrangements had been made by nightfall. He packed light—a ration of dried meat, a water skin, a bedroll, a makeshift torch, and his flint and steel were all that made the cut. Come first light, he had his sack slung over his shoulder and every intention of beginning on his journey.

There was but one thing that could weigh on his featherlight heart, and that was the compulsory walk past the boat in order to reach the wood's edge. There was no avoiding the judgmental glare of the skeleton that presided in its seemingly permanent resting spot beside his cabin, no obviating the deep-seated guilt that it called to the forefront of his mind.

This trip was a flagrant shirking of responsibility; at least two days worth of work would be lost to it, and that was only if he encountered no hiccups along the way. He adjusted the sack's strap and approached the incomplete vessel. Placing a hand on one of the smooth planks of wood, Theo tried to convince himself of an untruth—that his recent stagnation in regard to the progress on his boat had not been of his own doing, but that of mother nature's. It'd been the damages inflicted by the hail storm that had set him back, for he'd had no choice but to pry off the many damaged bits of wood and start from near scratch. But he couldn't even allow the excuses to settle in his mind before casting them all away; he was incapable of lying to himself any longer. Hail storm or not, he knew he had grown too lax in his work.

Perhaps his psyche would have shattered into a million little pieces had he let himself become entirely consumed with the construction of the boat, with sorting through the logistics of finding Clara. Part of him knew this to be true, and yet it didn't prevent the selfishness he felt.

Theo ran his palm through his hair, leaving it to stick out of his head at odd angles. He paced back and forth a few times, then he cursed and let the sack fall to the ground. Looking toward the woods, he wondered if Iris could see him from somewhere within the trees.

Would she ever be able to forgive him? He couldn't say, but he set to work on the boat anyway.

***

"I don't understand," Iris vociferated from beyond the door. "I finally offer you the very thing you've claimed time and time again to want, and—and *what*? Now it is no longer of value to you?"

"You've not gone to the caverns?" Theo asked. The fork he'd been using to eat clanged against his plate as he hastened to convey his body from where he sat at the little table to the place beside the door.

"Of course I haven't gone. What would have been the sense in that seeing as *you* did not go?"

So she had been watching him. Of course she had. He could not decide if he was more amused or perturbed by the fact.

"I'm sorry, Iris. But in all fairness, your terms weren't exactly easy to meet."

"My terms had been accepted," she quickly replied.

"I know. And that is why I apologize for not seeing through my end of the agreement. Besides, it is not as if I had agreed with the intent of abrogating."

"Why did you then?"

"I have other responsibilities, ones I have been sorely neglecting. It is my duty to do everything within my power to find Clara. Don't pretend to have forgotten. You yourself very recently reminded me of this obligation when you ordered me to finish my boat and leave."

Iris was suspiciously quiet for a time.

"Iris? Have you gone?"

"No," was her quiet reply. "I'm still here."

"I am sorry. Truly."

"Do not be."

He was stunned by the sudden realization that Iris had actually wanted him to go to the caverns. She had not made the arrangements to simply appease him, but also herself. A sense of panic surged through him as he considered her feelings as he never had before. For the first time, it seemed as if *he* had aggrieved *her*. His actions had made him appear indifferent when in truth he was anything but. He could not stand to have her think so poorly of him.

"Tomorrow. I will leave tomorrow morning, and I will fulfill my commitment of convening with you in the caverns." The vow pitched from Theo's lips the same way the gambling dice had been thrust from the hand of his father so many times before, with haste and foolishness.

"Tomorrow?" Iris asked, and the lightness in her voice wrought his next response.

"Yes, tomorrow. I give you my word."

Chapter Twenty-One

The remaining hours of the night hummed with palpable energy, but Theo forced his excitement down so that he might get a few hours of shut eye, for he had a long journey ahead of him come morning time.

Morning came as predicted, and Theo called Iris's directions back to the fore of his mind. He began to trace the pallid sun on its journey through the sky, hopeful that he might set foot on the beach before nightfall. This gave him no time to dally. Packing light had served him well, for he was able to maintain the necessary brisk pace with very little trouble.

Passing through the only substantial bit of woods on the entire island was no small feat by any means. Where much of the landscape was too rocky and frozen for the average sapling to break ground, this region had an abundant supply of rich soil, leaving it densely shrouded with evergreens that went as far as the eye could see.

Theo knew these were the very same woods he had gotten himself lost in, the ones Iris had mysteriously rescued him from, but he now saw them in an entirely different light. What had once been a dreary source of nightmares was now all things enchanting and whimsical.

His eyes drank in the many sights of the wood, devouring even the smallest of details with a voracious appetite. Within him lived the penetrating awareness that these would likely be his final sights before finally seeing her. Would he ever again be able to appreciate the silent beauty of a fresh blanket of snow or a copse of icicle adorned trees once he laid his eyes upon Iris? He must take some moments to notice these things now, for he anticipated they would soon be unable to arouse the same effect within him.

He ate as he walked to preserve time, stopping only when his legs gave him no choice but to do so. Before long something in the air shifted, and suddenly the smell of pine needles became something more briny, and the chirping of birds was drowned out by the sound of rolling tides. By the time he cleared through the last of the trees the sky was as ripe as a juicy plum, glinting with the first signs of stars. He could just vaguely make out his surroundings with the little remaining light.

To the north Theo spied the looming cliffs that Iris had denoted. He advanced toward them, relying on the shoreline to guide him when it grew too dark to make out their shadowed edges with any clarity.

The distinct sound of waves crashing against rock had been his only warning that he was coming near the cliff base. With his arm extended before him, he was soon able to locate a wall. It was cold and damp, coated with a thick layer of sludge. There he thought he could hear the faint trickling of water coming from somewhere within. He followed it blindly until the wall gave way to a gaping black hole—an entrance.

Setting down his pack, Theo withdrew his torch, and after a few moments of fumbling in the dark with the flint and steel he managed to generate an initial spark, and then a flame.

Engulfed in the torch's golden orb, he was able to see five or so feet in any direction, and so he began on the steep descent into the earth. On either side of him were crenulated walls of ashen stone, and up above hung hundreds of stalactites, so low in some places that he was forced to duck to avoid being impaled. The bone-chilling winds of the sea were replaced by a cool dampness that clung to him like a second skin. He suppressed a shiver and pressed on into the unknown, bolstered by the knowledge that Iris awaited him from somewhere within.

The subdued trickling soon became the reverberating rumble of water crashing upon water. Theo followed the sound. The farther he went, the more constricted he felt, and it was not mere claustrophobia of the mind that he was experiencing. The walls were quickly tapering into a passage so tight that, had it been a hair's breadth tighter, he would have had no choice but to turn back and find another way in. But just as he feared he might actually become wedged in the particularly narrow vestibule, the space abruptly opened up into a capacious chamber.

The source of all the splashing revealed itself here in the form of a cascading waterfall. Theo extended the torch as high as his arm could reach, but still he could not clearly see the origin of its torrents. Distracted by its sheer magnitude, Theo took no notice at all of the woman who watched him from below.

"Theo!" she called out over the din of the falls.

Startled to find that he was not as alone in the chamber as he'd thought, he nearly dropped his torch. But with a fleeting moment's notice, he got his wits about him and directed his attention to the place from which the voice had come, the voice he knew belonged to none other than Iris.

He was standing on the edge of a wide crag, some twenty feet above the reservoir into which the waterfall emptied itself, and there, bobbing atop those turbulent waters, was a small head. She was so distant that he could make out none of her features, appearing to him as more of a dark smudge than a human being.

"Iris! What are you doing down there?" Theo cried, rapidly ripping off layers of clothes with the intent to dive in after her.

"No! Stop! I'm okay! Just listen to me before you go doing anything rash!" Iris's urgent shout came from below.

Theo obeyed, pausing to hear what she might say next. "What is it, then?"

"You must head in that direction!" she called, gesturing to Theo's left. "Follow that path and you will come to a small pool! Things will be much quieter there!"

"Okay, fine," Theo nodded. "But, Iris, don't you think you should come out of the water? Perhaps we should walk together?"

Still Water

"No, you are too high up, anyhow! Don't worry, I swim quite well! Now go!" And without another word, Iris gracefully vanished beneath the water and swam away.

Theo was mystified to his very core, but he could only look on with his dumbfounded stare for so long. Eventually, he managed to shut his gaping mouth and commence down the path which Iris had dictated to him.

The distance to be traveled was much longer than he could have anticipated. But that very well may have been due to the fact that his every footfall had to be carefully considered, lest he should slip on a patch of loose gravel and take an undesired tumble from the elevated ridge upon which he walked. His torch was continually shifted from illuminating the ground beneath him to the darkness above, and his peripheral vision was inundated by the many menacing shadows looming on all sides. His flame, of course, revealed nothing more than oddly-shaped rock formations, but even once his eyes had discerned them, his mind still struggled to accept that they were slabs of stone and not cave raiders waiting to assail him in the dark.

In short, Theo was extremely on edge by the time he reached his destination, a grotto of sorts, it seemed.

While still quite spacious, it came nowhere near the size of the former chamber, likely due to the simple fact that this one seemed to house no imposing waterfalls. The only sound coming from within was the constant dripping of moisture from the tips of the stalactites overhead, a steady tempo that would do well to soothe Theo's nerves if he could ever calm his mind enough to focus on it. There was a large, solid platform of stone upon which he stood, which extended a good distance ahead to penetrate a naturally forming basin. Its water appeared inky, both from a general lack of light and from the wealth of limestone sediment that had loosened from the walls and ceiling.

Theo slowed his breaths, concentrating on his inhales and exhales as he tried to shift his brain out of survival mode, and he nearly ceased to breathe at all when he saw a shadow floating there amongst all the blackness.

Tentatively, Theo moved closer, raising his torch with the cautious intent to discern her image, quite the challenge given the substantial amount of space that still remained between them—he, at the precipice of the stone, and she, submerged in the pool of water a good fifteen feet away. Still, Theo was able to glimpse parts of her that he had never been privy to before. Large, dark eyes deeply set into a delicate, narrow face. High cheekbones and a clear, smooth brow. She was more beautiful than he could have ever imagined. And her lips, so supple. So…

"Iris!" Theo exclaimed in alarm. "You must be freezing. Your lips—they're turning blue!"

Those blue lips curved into a relaxed smile. "Be still, Theo. I am not freezing."

"But—"

"Sit, will you?"

Theo stammered for a moment, then acquiesced. "Will you not come sit beside me?"

"No, I will not."

"But I don't understand. That water must be as cold as ice. It simply cannot be good for your constitution to remain immersed in it for so long a time."

"I find it most curious, Theo," Iris mused. "The way you claim to know so little about me, yet somehow still manage to speak as if you know what I require better than myself."

He looked at her for a moment, but could not come up with any reasonable retort to her argument.

"So…" he began sheepishly. "It seems you have a propensity for the water then?"

"I do." She smiled again and Theo's heart fluttered like a caged bird. "It is where I've always belonged."

Despite his inability to grasp what her words truly meant, he could not help but hear the honesty in them, and therefore he experienced a strong sense of gratification at the fact that she could remain in her preferred element as they spoke.

"Then I suppose I am glad you are comfortable."

"And you? Are you comfortable?"

Theo chuckled. "I am sitting on a hard rock whose coldness I can feel straight through my trousers." His smile widened, becoming something more genuine. "But I am here. With you. And for that reason I will cease to complain any further."

"Do you find you're nervous?" she asked, tilting her head.

"I think I've made this moment so very large in my mind that it would be strange if I wasn't."

"So what do you think? Now that you're in the moment?" Her glistening, dark hair fanned out around her pale shoulders in a most mesmerizing way, rendering Theo speechless for a moment.

"I think... I think you are most exquisite," he stammered out. "Although I would not exactly claim to be able to *see* you under these circumstances." Theo squinted his eyes and extended his torch toward her to emphasize his point. "You are so far away and it is rather dark in this place."

"Yes," Iris said, and Theo waited for her to say more, to offer up some sort of excuse. She did no such thing.

"Do you not wish to come closer? Would you not like to get a better look at me?" Theo asked, his voice lilting in a bantering manner.

"I can see you quite well from here," Iris responded.

"And what is it you see?"

"A human."

"Ah, so I see we're getting quite specific, are we?"

"What I see is a human man..." She seemed to hesitate, her shameless smile tapering off of her lips, her eyes large and earnest. "A human man that has been... *kind* to me."

Theo was surprised by her response. He took a moment to allow it to settle before again speaking. "It's only fair that I should return the kindness you've extended to me."

Something shifted in Iris's expression.

"You think I am kind?" she asked, her voice strained.

Theo's brows knit together. "Of course I do. Your kindness is unmatched in my eyes. I've attempted to convey my gratitude to you before, but perhaps I should have made things more clear. Iris, without you I don't think I would have survived. And it is not mere fish and medicine I am speaking of now. It goes beyond that. It always has."

Something strange was happening inside of Iris. It was almost as if a piece of herself had been severed by Theo's admission, though she knew not what this piece might represent to her.

"Theo, will you blow out your torch?"

"What? Why? If I do, we'll be left in complete darkness."

"Do you trust me?"

And it was his trust that led him to do as she asked and put out the flame.

"Stay where you are," Iris said into the dark. "You have no reason to fear." Her voice was closer now. With no knowledge of what she planned to do, Theo stiffened in anticipation. "I'm right here," she whispered, and then she brought her hand to his.

Her hand moved until their palms were flush together, his calluses scraping gently over her smoothness.

"I've never found pleasure in physical touch before, not in the way... others seem to," Iris breathed. "I suppose I simply wanted to try it. To see what it is like."

Theo persisted in his stillness, refusing to yield to the intense urge to touch her more, to let his hands take over and roam where they so wished to. "And?" he asked her in a gravelly voice.

"I think it is nice," she said, pressing the pads of her fingers into his. He pushed back, earning from her a little giggle. He instinctively curled his fingers to entwine them with hers, but found he was physically prevented from doing so. Theo's fingers had come into contact with the thin webs of skin that stretched between her own, and he issued a strange noise of innocent surprise. The water splashed, breaking the silence as Iris quickly pulled away.

"Wait!" Theo cried. "I'm sorry. Please, come back."

She was so quiet he could no longer tell if she was still there or if he was now alone in the lightless grotto.

"Please, Iris," he pleaded. "Please come back."

A moment later he felt her touch once more, tentative and timid. A warm rush of relief flooded through him. She spread her fingertips then, an invitation for Theo to explore if he so wished. His gentle fingers ran over the sensitive fibers of flesh. A shiver coursed through her as his skin moved over hers.

"You were born with these?" he asked softly.

"Yes."

"Is this the reason you feel you belong in the water?"

She considered his question for a moment. "I suppose it is a part of the reason," she conceded.

His fingers caressed hers in their completeness with a tenderness she'd never before known.

"I like them," he murmured. "They're soft, like rose petals."

Iris smiled, and on that night two hands would remain as one.

Chapter Twenty-Two

The world around Theo seemed impossibly dark, and there was a brief moment when he wondered if he'd only dreamed he opened his eyes.

Reaching up to touch his own face, he confirmed two things—he was really awake and his eyes were really open. His chest swelled with panic for an instant before his memory returned to him.

"Iris?" he whispered.

There came no reply.

Sitting up, he felt around for his torch, then felt around some more until his fingers happened upon the pack which held his flint and steel. He struggled blindly to forge the necessary spark, but soon managed. There, beneath the flickering glow of torchlight, he was able to confirm that the grotto was no longer graced by Iris's presence.

In her absence, she'd seen fit to leave behind a trail of breadcrumbs—or pebbles, rather—so as to aid Theo in tracing his way back to the outer-world. Iris and her strange ways at work once again. Theo smiled as he packed away his things, wishing she would have simply woke him so that they might leave together, but then he supposed that wouldn't have been very characteristic of her. In fact if Theo had come to know anything of Iris at all, then he would have guessed she was somewhere close by, watching him at that very moment.

"Thank you," he said to the darkness. "Please, do come and see me once we're back home." But for some reason he felt as if he had misspoken, so he corrected himself by adding, "Once I've made it back to the cabin, I mean."

Still Water

It was midday by the time Theo finally emerged from the caverns, and he hiked until sundown. At about the halfway point he settled in for the night, situating his meager camp in some nondescript part of the woods. A small fire and a paltry dinner of dried meat would hold him over for the night.

Tucked comfortably into his bedroll, Theo gazed up toward the night sky. It was fractured into segments by the treetops, an optical illusion to make something so large seem slightly more fathomable. The longer he looked, the more his mind struggled to comprehend such great vastness. He could run for his entire life and, still, he would remain under this same exact sky. Some things were truly inescapable. The stars twinkled sweetly, reminding him of how the torchlight had reflected off of the two dark pools that were Iris's eyes. Those eyes were very much like the night sky, Theo thought to himself. He would never escape them.

The sun was at its peak when the settlement came into view the following day. Though he was admittedly exhausted, he felt relieved to see so many familiar sights after days spent in unfamiliar places. The singed cabins and the dilapidated chicken coop, even the Mourner now brought him an unexpected sense of comfortability. It made him reflect on how long he'd been here. The month was now February by his count, putting him somewhere around eight weeks on the island.

That was a harsh reality for Theo to face.

Once inside his cabin, he slung the pack off of his back and laid himself down on the thin straw mattress with a grunt. When, exactly, had these four walls stopped feeling like a temporary means of survival and begun to feel so much like his own? Was it after making the repairs? Or when he'd begun to fill it up with all the practical bits and bobs he found throughout the settlement? Or was it the simple fact that he'd been sleeping beneath this same roof night after night? It was when his eyes came to the door that he understood the true answer.

That evening he waited beside that very door, this time positioning himself on the outside of it. Things had changed between himself and Iris, of that he was certain. The barrier was now a thing of the past, obsolete.

He waited in earnest, eyes scanning the treeline again and again, but his wait would be in vain. She would not come, not on this night.

Theo was not necessarily wrong in his initial sentiments—things *had* changed, and they both cared deeply for one another—but he still had a fundamental misunderstanding when it came to Iris. The more she came to value Theo, the less she valued herself. In fact, she was beginning to develop a keen dislike for the things that made her so... *other*, for these were the very things she believed would turn Theo away from her if he were to discover them.

He had been kind to her about her webbed fingers, but she was not deluded. His kindness would not—*could* not—transcend so far as to allow him to accept her in her completeness. And so instead of going to Theo as he sat out in the cold on that night, she became consumed with her own personal pursuits.

For hours on end she would run the tip of her tongue over her serrated teeth until it bled. She obsessively picked at the scales that ran along her midsection and arms. She directed every ounce of disgust and loathing at her muscular tail and the gills that flanked either side of her neck. Soon this strong aversion toward her own anatomy compelled her to go against her nature, to spend less and less time in the water, and as a result, her body began to undergo a strange transformation.

Her gills, dry as bone, began to seal themselves, and her irritated scales finally began to scab over with fresh flesh. Her chafed tongue had succeeded in rubbing her teeth into flat nubs, and her webs slowly melted away from the spaces between her fingers.

With saint-like patience, Iris waited for the final stage of her metamorphosis—the parting of her tail. Its death proved most challenging of all. It was a great many days spent writhing in pain as her bone structure shifted, as muscle, sinew, and skin split apart only to fuse again around a new and unfamiliar framework.

Still Water

It was an ordinary day in the first week of March when Iris had finally been reborn.

Like a newborn calf on her wobbly legs she stumbled over the melting snow, finding Theo in front of his cabin, busy at work putting the finishing touches on his boat. Skin bare beneath the cool shade of the spruce trees, Iris collapsed at his feet.

Overcome with confusion, he stood in place, looking dumbly at the body on the ground. It was the single article she wore on her body that shook him from his stupor—the necklace he had made with his own hands, a pearl hanging from her neck by a leather cord. With a start, he realized that this was *Iris* who lay crumpled on the ground like a rag doll. Iris, who he thought had gone from his life, never to return.

His hammer fell from his hand with a thud and he took her quickly into his arms, delivering her into the cabin.

Chapter Twenty-Three

It would be a full three days before Iris woke. The moment her eyes fluttered open, Theo insisted she eat and drink before anything else. The meat and water that would have once repulsed her now brought about an acute hunger that burned deep in her core. She partook of it with unanticipated fervor. The lightness in her head relented at last, but her body remained weak and foreign to her.

"How do you feel?" Theo asked when she finished her meal. He had watched her the entire time she ate with wide, disbelieving eyes. It was as if he were still trying to work out if she was truly there or if this was all just some sort of cruel trick.

"Not very well," was Iris's reply, and it was the truth. She felt achy and fatigued, scarcely able to even recollect the events of the past weeks in which she had undergone her bizarre transfiguration. Everything was a bit hazy, her literal vision along with her memory blurred at the edges.

"You must continue to rest," Theo said with conviction, though his bewilderment would not quite renounce itself from his expression.

At least now he could account for her absence. A month had passed since they'd seen each other last, and over time he'd come to the logical conclusion that she must have left the caverns underwhelmed and so decided to cease contact with him entirely.

To now find out he had been wrong was like sustaining an arrow through the chest. She'd been sick, indisposed, and all the while he'd been working on his boat so that he might put this island—and Iris—behind him once and for all.

He berated his objective mind, but praised his wounded heart for impeding his productivity, because the truth was that the boat should never have taken four weeks to finish. There had been a mere week's worth of work remaining at the time of Iris's disappearance, but whenever he came too close to completion, he would find another tweak to be made. Anything to prolong his departure. He would never have admitted it to himself at the time, but he'd always known he was holding out hope that Iris would come back to him.

"I should have foreseen that you would fall ill after swimming in those freezing waters," he muttered, more to himself than to her. "I should have looked for you."

"I told you I didn't want to be found." Her voice sounded so frail that it brought tears to his eyes.

"I will never have the words to tell you how very sorry I am," he said, reaching for her hand. When their fingers interlaced, he felt the absence of her webs. His brow scrunched as he drew her hand out from beneath the blanket.

"Your fingers…"

"Yes. They're like yours now," Iris finished his thought for him.

"But how?"

"I'm not certain. The webs were gone when I woke."

Gently, he led her hand toward him so he could get a better look. He caught the briefest glimpse of red flesh between each of her fingers, tender and raw, before something in his expression made her self-conscious enough to snatch her hand away.

"Iris, what was that?"

She attempted to avert her gaze, and the motion revealed those very same marks on the side of her neck, marks that appeared like wounds very recently healed. As his eyes traveled to where a loose linen shirt had slid down past her shoulders, he saw more of them on her upper chest. Something inside of Theo plummeted like a heavy stone. In his rush to protect her dignity, he had covered her the moment he got her inside. Haste had caused him to overlook the many welts strewn across her skin. He felt sick to his stomach.

"Has someone hurt you?" The words came out strangled, as if he had to wrench each one out with force.

From Iris came no answer.

"Iris, if someone has done something to you, you must tell me."

His curt tone made her nervous, and the expression on his face was one she had never before seen. "Are you angry with me?" she asked him.

At once, everything about him softened. "Angry with *you*? What? No, of course not."

He brought his hand to her temple and she found herself leaning into his touch. Looking into her dark, starry eyes, Theo decided he would never ask her about it again. Whatever had happened to her out there, they would escape it together. He would make sure of it.

"It's okay," he whispered into her hair. "Everything will be okay. I promise you this."

A day had passed since Iris had awoken from her long sleep, and she'd finally talked Theo into allowing her out of bed.

"If what you say is true, I must be able to get around on my own." It was the boat she was speaking of, finally fit for sailing. They were finally going to leave.

"I would carry you wherever we went if need be," Theo declared triumphantly.

"And I would never allow it, even if you would. I am not a helpless damsel from one of your many fairy tales."

They smiled at each other. Theo was glad that despite everything, Iris had been able to cling to her strong sense of vitality and spirit. He offered her his hand and she took it, letting the blanket fall away from her shoulders.

When her bare legs shifted out into the open, Theo instinctively averted his eyes. He'd never gotten around to fully dressing her, had he? At the time of her arrival, he'd simply tugged the shirt from his own back and slipped it over her head before tucking her into bed.

This moment—the one where she'd rise from her stint of rest so scantily clad—had completely slipped his mind.

"What is it? What's the matter?" he heard her say.

With his back to her, Theo quickly assembled what he thought would best suit Iris from his limited wardrobe. A thick woolen shirt, his cleanest pair of trousers, and a rope to hold them up around her waist.

"Here," he said gruffly.

"Theo," Iris whispered. "What is wrong? Why won't you look at me?"

"It would be most... impolite of me." His voice was strained and stiff, his head still lowered as he waited for her to take the clothing from his outstretched hand.

"What? Why, that is the most foolish thing I've ever heard."

"Iris, I will look at you once you have dressed yourself," Theo said firmly.

She scoffed, baffled once more by humans and their many odd rules and rituals. But she accepted the pile of fibers from him nonetheless, surprised to find that she was actually *cold*.

She decided to begin with the trousers, but the mechanics of her legs were still so novel to her, and she stumbled as she attempted to piece together how exactly she was to put them on.

Before she could even comprehend that she was falling, Theo was there. His arms wrapped around her naturally, as if he'd already done so a thousand times before. She could feel his chest heaving against her own as she lifted her chin to face him. His stormy eyes were darker than usual when she looked into them. They searched her face, an unanswered question in them.

"Are you all right?" he asked her.

She merely looked at him for a moment, stunned. They were so close she could feel the warmth of his breath on her cheeks.

"Yes. I think so," Iris replied, unexpectedly winded.

"Would you like some help?" Theo asked quietly, keeping his gaze on her face.

Her only reply was a single, quick nod.

Theo took a careful step back, keeping his hands on Iris's shoulders to steady her. He tried not to notice her body's silhouette through the shirt's threadbare material, the way the curve of her hip led to the slope of her thighs. Tried not to think of the softness of her skin as he knelt before her, gently wrapping a large hand around her ankle to guide it through the first leg of the pants. Tried to steady his quickening pulse as he caught her gazing down at him, a look of wonder upon her angelic face.

Slowly he rose, and Iris swore she could feel the heat of him travel up her body, though not a single inch of his skin touched her own as he moved. Suddenly, she was starkly aware of the way he towered over her, his height never before feeling so pronounced as in this moment.

"Iris."

"Yes," she breathed.

"Turn around, please."

She obeyed, angling her head so she could still see him out of the corner of her eye. She soon felt the slight pressure of his fingers on her wrists, lifting them. Then the feathery sensation of her shirt gliding across her skin, up and over her head.

Theo's eyes trailed down Iris's bare back, a newfound hunger in them. Without thought, he leaned forward, allowing his lips to brush against the supple skin of her neck, the pink welts that would torment him until they healed over once and for all.

Iris's breath caught, and she melted into Theo's touch. His kisses traveled down, over her shoulder and onto her collarbone, at which Iris let out a stifled moan.

Theo remembered himself then, and despite the all-consuming part of him that begged for more, urging him to bring forth all the various beautiful sounds that Iris might make for him, he forced his fist to close around the woolen shirt. He then pulled it over her head, untucking her silken hair from its collar to let it fall once more around her shoulders. Then he stepped away.

"Theo…" Iris began.

"This will do for now," he said quickly. "Perhaps I will be able to find something of a better fit in one of the other cabins."

Iris turned around, looking at him through heavy lids, though he refused to meet her gaze.

"Theo."

He began to busy himself with re-arranging the stack of firewood that sat beside the hearth.

"In fact, I should go check now. I believe I may have seen something in—"

"*Theo.*"

He stilled then, allowing her to come to him. Shame washed through him, so strong he could scarcely look her in the eye.

"I apologize—for my blatant lack of prudence. I don't know what came over me. It was a terribly foul—"

She placed a fingertip on his lips to quiet him.

"What do you call that? That thing you've just done with your lips," she whispered, looking to the place where her finger rested, eyes glinting with something Theo could not quite name.

He hesitated, running a hand through his tousled hair.

"I… I kissed you," he finally said.

"Do it again," Iris commanded so softly that he thought he may have misheard her.

"What?"

"I said I want you to do it again. I want you to kiss me."

And so he did.

***

Iris's head rested soundly against Theo's chest. They were in bed, the cabin lit by the light of a single fluttering candle.

"In all the excitement of our afternoon," Iris began, a cheeky grin on her face, "you forgot to tell me where we will soon be off to."

Theo shifted, rustling the many blankets he'd draped over them to keep warm.

"Where we will be off to?" he asked through a yawn. His mind was yet consumed with things such as warmth and stillness and slumber.

"Yes, our destination. Where will we be sailing on that boat of yours?"

Iris thought of all the places they might go together, the human life she would now be able to lead alongside Theo.

"Well, we will go to the Horned Isle, I suppose. Once you are better."

"The Horned Isle?"

"Mhm," he hummed groggily. "To find Clara." And though sleep hung quite heavily on him in that moment, Theo felt the weight of confession being lifted. Saying those simple words aloud to Iris made them into a tangible thing. A reality that did not quite exist before that moment.

Iris curled her legs into her chest. "Yes. Of course," was all she said.

And as Theo stood out in the open for all to see, Iris receded farther into the ramparts of dishonesty.

Chapter Twenty-Four

Theo was seated at the table, staring vacantly through the window toward the boat. It was small, but sufficient for accommodating two people and enough supplies to carry them through a few weeks at sea. The thought of weathering those wide open waters so soon twisted his stomach into knots. Though he felt some degree of confidence in his knowledge of the fundamentals of sailing from his years at sea, he had never before put it to the test, always trusting his father's crew to see to such matters. If only he'd been able to foresee his current situation, then perhaps he would have spent less time with his nose stuck in his books and more time manning the lines when the stakes hadn't been so high.

However, it was thanks to those books that he had knowledge of the "spritsail," a type of sail most convenient for smaller vessels, such as his skiff. And so he'd done his best to rig the four-sided strip of canvas based on a memory of what he'd read so long ago. When they reached the Horned Isle perhaps there would be a knowledgeable seaman who could tell Theo if he'd managed well.

"It needs a name," Theo said suddenly, jarring Iris from her own contemplations at her usual spot by the hearth.

"What does?"

"The boat. We should name her before we take her out to sea."

"Why would one give a name to an inanimate object?"

Theo thought about it. "It proves a sailor takes pride in their vessel, I suppose."

Pride, an emotion that still made such little sense to Iris. In the natural world, pride did not exist; there was no room for it. Death always awaited those who clung to such foolish ideals.

Still, she humored Theo, naming the boat "Serpent of the Sea" to pay homage to all she had forsaken, hoping that her intuition had not been lost along with her claws and teeth.

Theo reverted to gazing out the window and Iris wondered what he might be thinking of. He had very recently come to the decision that they would not leave the island until they both felt certain she was well enough to endure prolonged exposure to the elements. If she was to be honest, Iris thought she could have managed the trip just fine in her current state. She was weak, yes, but weak in comparison to what she had once been. The way she felt now was likely how most human beings felt on a daily basis. There was but one reason for Iris to portray herself as one still on the mend, and that was her realization that she had no wish to leave.

Theo's talk of finding Clara had affirmed to her that the island was their sanctuary, a place where the two of them could live together in peace and solitude.

Iris never corrected Theo in his assumption that someone had hurt her; it was too convenient an explanation for her many blemishes, for her supposed weakness. And so he had taken on the unspoken role of being her protector, a duty that seemed to bring him that fatuous sense of pride that humans seemed to be in perpetual pursuit of.

Though she did not like to withhold so much truth from him, she did so only to protect him from the sadness he would find if they left. Perhaps if he could find a sense of purpose for himself here—even if Iris had to fabricate it for him—he would finally feel happy.

That was what she wanted after all, for Theo to be happy, no matter the cost.

He began to speak of Edris more during this contrived period of wait, opening up about the man that was more of a father than the one who had sired him. And how fascinating the connection forged between these two humans was! Most curious of all was the way it seemed to pain Theo to speak of Edris, but his insistence on doing so anyways. He *wanted* this pain, injuring himself intentionally just so that he might remember things about this man—the conversations they had, the experiences they shared.

Iris had always assumed that when one died, they were gone, entirely ceasing to exist. But perhaps that was not always the case.

It brought about thoughts of the fish eggs, the ones she had taken such a liking to in the past. How, clustered together for an ephemeral moment of time before hatching, they too forged their own kind of kinship.

"What is it like to have a sister?" she found herself asking Theo.

A flash of hurt came over his face, but Iris thought perhaps it would help him to remember about Clara, the same way it helped him to remember about Edris.

"It's a difficult thing to describe." He looked into the distance as he worked to corral so many swirling thoughts and feelings. "It is a great burden, having a sibling. You share so much with them. A childhood, an upbringing, a womb. To have a sibling is to share half of everything. And so naturally you begin to feel as if you bear some sort of responsibility to ensure that they get something from it all, from this life, and if you fail—" His voice broke off and he looked at the floor, wiping his nose. A moment passed. Theo sniffled and nodded. "It is a great burden. But it is also the greatest gift. I have never known a greater gift than sharing half of everything with Clara."

Iris didn't know if she had any siblings, but for the first time she considered the possibility of such a thing. She thought of a piece of herself out there somewhere, living an entirely separate life that she would never know of. What a powerful thing it would be, Iris thought, to share half of an existence with another. Had she stolen that away from Theo? Could such a thing be stolen at all?

Perhaps that was what she and Theo were doing right now—sharing their existences. The thought excited her, encouraged her to cling to him even tighter.

***

It seemed wise that they should try to persist on fresh meat while they still remained on the island so that they might store the rest of the dried meat for the trip. With Iris now too weak to do any fishing, Theo decided to put his own skills to work, setting some snares along the outskirts of the woods. Iris decided to accompany him in checking on them, claiming she could do with some fresh air and exercise.

It was uncommonly warm for March in such northerly regions, and the many layers of snow and ice on the lowlands of the island had melted away completely to reveal tufts of dormant brown grass below. The skies shone as blue as hand-painted porcelain plates, and dappled sunlight rained down onto Theo and Iris's faces as they walked side by side.

They found the first snare empty. Theo grunted, but was otherwise unperturbed.

"Don't worry, there are plenty more for us to check. I'm sure one of them has snagged us a squirrel or rabbit by now," he assured Iris, who was peering down at the snare with overly-suspicious eyes.

She may have relinquished her tail, but she now had proof that her instincts had not deserted her after all, for they were the reason she'd inspected the empty snare for a fraction of a moment longer than Theo. If it hadn't been for the gentle springtime breeze, she likely would not have found anything amiss, even in those extra lingering seconds. But like a willful ally, the wind took hold of the faintly floating scent and delivered it directly to the blunted nerves within her nostrils, activating their muscle memory and triggering her alarm. It was not the noxious reek of animal that she smelled, nor was it the piquant essence of human, but something much more obscure. Something that was distinctly familiar yet somehow still uncharted to her, as if by some sort of distant olfactory memory.

Still crouched beside the snare, Iris turned her gaze back toward Theo. On her face she wore a mask of cool composure.

"Yes, I'm sure you're right," was her response.

She stood and wiped her hands on her trousers, attempting to give Theo a reassuring smile, though she couldn't be sure as to whether it was truly convincing. Her mind was consumed with trying to deduce who or what had touched that snare before she and Theo arrived. The scent she picked up had been fresh, likely shed sometime within the last twenty-four hours.

The two of them walked on, Theo speaking fondly of the pleasant weather that Iris would now be incapable of enjoying. She was instead burdened by the sinister feeling that they were being watched, though her own eyes could not pinpoint the perpetrator. By the time they reached the final snare, whose knot had snagged for them a particularly fat weasel, she was certain that something was very, very wrong. The scent she had caught a small whiff of earlier now permeated the air around them with a great heaviness. Wherever they went it seemed to follow, but its source remained otherwise undetectable to her.

They soon returned to the cabin for dinner. Iris's grumbling stomach had gone sour, making it difficult to eat very much.

"Are you all right?" Theo had asked her after watching her push the meat around with her fork for some time.

"Yes, I'm fine. Just a bit tired I think."

Theo's gray eyes clouded with worry. "Would you like to lie down for a bit?"

She looked down at her food, her smooth brow creasing.

"Iris, you mustn't force yourself to finish if you've no appetite for it. I'll take no offense. Honest." A small smile played upon the curve of his lips, though the clouds in his eyes did nothing to disperse. She smiled back at him and carefully laid the fork down on her plate.

"Here, I'll wash up." Theo stood to take her plate. "Why don't you go get some rest?"

"No!" She nearly leapt from her chair. Theo regarded her with wide eyes. "I'll do the washing today," she mumbled, shrugging her shoulders the way she'd seen Theo do whenever he was trying to appear indifferent. "It's the least I can do."

"Sure," he said, watching her doubtfully as she quickly gathered the plates and silverware in her arms. "Are you certain you're all right?"

"Of course. I'm just craving a bit more fresh air after my meal," she assured him. "Will you be so kind as to light a fire? The warmth always helps me sleep, and I do plan to lie down upon my return."

Theo set to work on kindling a flame while Iris went out the door, dishes in hand. She walked toward the canal, to the spot where they typically rinsed their tableware after meals. Before lowering herself to the ground, she cast one last look toward the cabin, just to be sure that Theo had not attempted to follow her. Satisfied that he remained safe within the walls of their home, she turned her attention back to the water, where a pair of black eyes looked back at her.

At first she thought it was merely her own reflection, but this water was far too agitated to act as a mirror. Iris watched in confusion as the face ascended until it broke through the swirling surface. Then she fell backwards, mouth agape, as she tried to understand what it was she saw. It was as if everything she had ceded in order to be with Theo had reassembled itself to stand before her.

Iris made to scramble away, glancing back toward the cabin. In her lapse of attention, the thing in the water lashed forward and grabbed a hold of her head.

"You," it said, voice mangled and warped. "You filthy disgrace."

"What? What are you?" Iris gasped, digging her fingers into the hard dirt at the canal's edge to keep from plunging into the water.

The creature wrenched Iris's face toward its own, lips spread in a wicked smile to reveal a set of pointed teeth. Then it laughed, or at least that's what Iris thought the grating noise emitting from its throat must have been.

"What am I, you ask?"

Iris struggled to free herself from its grasp.

"Look at me!" it growled. "Don't you see? Can't you see what I am?"

"I know what you are," Iris spat, trying and failing to avert her eyes from that dreadful face.

"Say it. I want to hear the words come from those pretty lips of yours."

"Let go of me."

"*Tell me!*" it commanded. "Tell me or I will do as you ask and release you, and then I will have him instead." Two hollow eyes flickered to the place behind Iris, to the cabin.

"Wait! No! Please," Iris pleaded.

It looked back at her in disgust. "Look at you, you vile, blubbering creature. How you beg—and for the worthless life of a human, no less! You will tell me now. Tell me what you think I am."

"Me," Iris squeaked.

It cocked its head like a hungry vulture. "I cannot hear you. Speak with purpose, weakling. Or have you already forgotten how?"

"You are me."

The most vile of smiles spread over the monster's face.

"You are all my worst parts," Iris went on, "all the parts I've ripped from myself and cast away into oblivion. My darkness."

"And what is left of you without me? Naught but a sniveling, sapless mess."

Iris glared at the abomination, revolted by what she saw. She hated it, hated herself.

"You think you are special now, don't you?" her darkness crooned, as if speaking to a naive child. "You think you've done something worthwhile? Make no mistake—you're not the first to have done this, to have torn yourself to pieces, to have made yourself into something so very small in the hope of finding acceptance. You stupid girl. You may have the skin, the teeth, the legs of a human, but you will never be one. You still have a rotten soul, and it will eat that human heart of yours alive."

"You know nothing of my soul!"

"Oh, you poor, poor child. You still don't understand. You were made to destroy, not to love. You will remember soon enough."

Iris's darkness then pressed its cold, dead lips to her own before descending back into the murky water.

Iris sat with her knees buried in the dirt, hand over her chest as she waited for her gasping breaths to subside. When she heard the cabin door open behind her, she piled up the dishes and stood.

"Iris, what—"

"All is well." She hurried toward him, eager to get them both as far away as possible from the canal.

"But I could've sworn I heard something."

Iris placed a hand on his arm in an attempt to turn him around. "We should get back inside."

Now he looked at her, frowning. "The dishes..." he began. Iris looked down and realized she hadn't gotten a chance to wash them. "Are you sure you're all right?"

"Yes, I've never been better. Now please, Theo, can we go inside?" She tugged on his sleeve and began walking. Thankfully, he followed.

When the door had been latched behind them, Theo took the dishes from Iris's hands and placed them on the table. Then he turned back to her, gently grasping the place between her shoulders and elbows.

"Will you tell me what happened now?" he asked. Iris's eyes flickered toward the door, like she was afraid of something beyond it. Theo's heart clenched as he noticed how her bottom lip trembled, how her eyes seemed to beg for comfort.

"What has frightened you so?" he commanded in a whisper. "You must tell me so I can prevent it from ever happening again."

"I..." Iris began in a shrunken voice. "I cannot."

Theo would not force her to divulge what had happened there by the canal, not when she was still so visibly shaken. So he did the only thing he could do at that moment. He held her. Her body went limp in his arms.

Though she was very nearly human, Iris was not yet human enough to cry genuine tears. Still, her body jostled with unrestrained sobs.

Iris had never experienced such a thing before this moment, and she quickly decided that crying, even without the tears, was not something she enjoyed. She despised the way her face swelled and the frightening sensation of being unable to catch her breath. But she reminded herself that she hated It infinitely more. She would choose these inconvenient human maladies a million times over if she could only remain with Theo and keep that monster as far from them as possible.

He tried his best to soothe her, running his hands over her slick black hair, whispering reassurances in her ear.

"Don't worry. I will never let anything hurt you again," he uttered.

Iris pulled her head away from his chest. Her eyes were rimmed with red, her forehead lined with worry. "It is not myself I fear for," she said. "It's you."

Chapter Twenty-Five

The days that followed were fraught with anxiety and indecision. Iris insisted they both stay in the cabin, all but barricading them inside. A chair wedged beneath the doorknob and the curtains drawn closed quickly became the new norm. As usual, remaining indoors for so long left Theo wound tight, and Iris's refusal to give him any indication as to why they must do so was growing rather tiresome. He only wished to help, but how could he when she would not tell him what the danger was?

Had he been granted the opportunity to doubt Iris's sanity, he very well may have. But he was afforded no such chance, for every night they heard the shuffling near the windows, the knocks on the walls, the jiggling of the doorknob. Whenever it began, Theo would leap to his feet and rush toward the door with intent to drive off whatever animal it was that frightened Iris so. But he still carried the burden of guilt in his heart for abandoning her once before, and it was for that reason that he found it exceedingly difficult to refuse her desperate pleas for him to stay by her side.

For what felt like an eternity, Theo went against his roaring instinct to confront and protect as Iris trembled in his arms, and no matter how much he begged to know the true nature of her fears she continued to rebuff him, simply insisting that they must stay inside regardless of the cost on his pride.

Soon the bed had been dragged away from the windows and walls, left in the center of the cabin's singular room. On one particular night, as they lay within its warmth, a voice came from beyond the draped window. *Iris's* voice.

"Theo," it called. "Theo, help me!"

Iris clutched at him hard enough to leave behind welts on his skin.

"What is that?" Theo asked, fear sinking into his most remote parts as he came to realize this was no mere animal, but something far more nefarious.

When Iris offered no answer, Theo threw the blanket off and rose. "Stay here. I'm going to see what's out there."

"No! Theo, you can't!"

"But I must! Or you must tell me what you know! What is this *thing* that prowls beyond our door? This evil, monstrous thing! It's speaking, using your voice, for goodness' sake! How can you expect me to just sit here while it plays with us like a cat with its mice? No, something must be done."

"Yes," the voice outside purred. "You're right, something must be done, indeed. Come outside, Theo. Leave behind your deceiver and open your eyes to the truth."

"Don't." Iris was standing now, both of her hands wrapped around Theo's wrist. "Please."

Theo's conviction weakened under her soft gaze. "Tell me what's out there," he said.

Iris looked toward the window, cloaked by the heavy drape. Her mind oscillated between telling him all or nothing, ultimately falling somewhere in between.

"It is the thing that hurt me before we found each other again," she whispered. Theo's face twisted into a visage of fury and he turned toward the door once more. Iris tugged him back toward her. "I thought it was gone. I thought we'd be safe at last–happy, even. But it followed me here. And now everything is coming apart. Nothing is as it should be and I can't understand why. I thought I did everything right. I thought–"

Theo enveloped her in his embrace.

"Hush now," he murmured. "This isn't your fault. We will stay here for one last night. Tomorrow, we leave this place and its many miseries behind."

Iris swore she could feel the creature's grim satisfaction seeping in through the walls and windows, invisible fumes come to poison their minds against each other.

That night, as Theo slept soundly, Iris could not manage to quiet her thoughts. Theo meant to leave tomorrow, and she couldn't exactly blame him. After all, it seemed the rational thing to do. But he didn't understand. How could he? He had no way of knowing that this thing–this *beast*–would stop at nothing to get what it wanted. It would follow them over land and sea, through blizzard and drought, until it had them both in its clutches. And what could she do to stop it? She'd given everything to be with Theo, but now it seemed she had to decide what she'd give to keep him.

Iris shifted her body, moving a pillow into her place in bed beside Theo so as not to disturb him. She held her breath until she could be certain he wouldn't stir from his slumber, then she tiptoed to the door, where she quietly relocated all the various objects they'd used to lock themselves in, and she let herself out into the coolness of the night.

She proceeded toward the canal, where she saw the creature limned by bleached moonlight. It was as if the beast had been expecting Iris, as if it had been waiting for this moment all along.

"We both know how this ends, do we not?" its wicked voice coiled into the shadows.

"I cannot say I do."

"Oh, don't pretend you forfeited your brain along with your tail. You know exactly what I'm going to say. It's time you give him up. Let him go. Release yourself from this inane burden and return to where you belong. Here, with me."

"I will never—" Iris growled.

It raised its claw as if to silence her. "You are a fool. He does not belong to you. Not now, not ever. Child, think—would he remain if he knew what you really are? He does not love you, he thinks you are a monster. I heard him say the words himself, we both did."

A smug smile crept over its face as Iris shook her head, trying to convince herself it wasn't true.

"You will release him either way. Send him away or I will have him."

"No!"

"I grow hungrier by the minute, my dear. I'm sure you remember how strong the urges are. You have until sunrise to decide *how* you wish to rid yourself of your precious pet."

"Wait, that's not enough time. Please!"

"Time? Oh, yes. That silly human concept. Never cared much for it myself." And the creature cackled with cruelty and malice until its head was fully submerged beneath the water.

Chapter Twenty-Six

Iris knew she should go inside; after all, these would be her final moments with Theo before she sent him off at the creature's behest. Instead she found herself resting on the doorstep, reminiscing on all the times she had sat in this very spot to talk with a human she held most dear to her on the other side.

How could it have come to this, she wondered. Theo's fairy tales had somehow led her to believe that if people did the right thing, if they were good and true, everything would work out for the best. So where had they gone wrong? Theo was good, of that Iris had no doubt. So maybe it was she who had fouled it all up. Maybe the creature was right, and her soul would always be rotten no matter how hard she tried.

An hour or so before the sun would crest over the horizon, Iris sighed deeply and stood. She could avoid it no longer.

Inside, Theo still slept. Despite her sadness, Iris could not resist smiling down at him. His simple innocence was most pronounced when he slept, a sight most beautiful to her. She closed her eyes, then, and listened. His soft breaths were rhythmic, like an incantation. A song that stirred her soul. Next, she inhaled his freshness, the scent both different and the same with her new sense of smell. Nostalgic, yet new, like treading an untouched path in a familiar forest. Finally, she lightly traced the curve of his cheek with her finger, thereby causing his eyes to open. Iris watched as the blurred edges of sleep began to clear from his countenance, and upon recognizing her Theo smiled languidly.

She tried her best to take this moment and bottle it within her mind, where its memory might be allowed to exist, preserved, safe. Could she at least have that? Or would this too be ripped from her?

She turned away from him, unable to face him any longer.

"What's happened?" he asked, bracing himself up on his elbows. "Is everything all right?"

She gave a small, rapid nod, but then her features crumpled and her cheeks flushed red. Her starry eyes would have shone with tears had she had any to give, but alas she did not. The lack thereof only served as a reminder of how wrong everything was.

"Theo," Iris began. "What do people do when things have become very, very unfair? When they are faced with great injustice?"

He stood, taking note of how the front door hung open on its hinges. Milky moonlight poured into the dark room, producing a halo of white around Iris's raven hair.

"They set to making things right," Theo answered.

There was fear in Iris's eyes—pure, undiluted fear.

"That... that *thing* wants to separate us," she said.

"I won't let it," Theo declared.

Iris took Theo's hand in hers, remembering the first time she'd done so beneath a shroud of darkness. That had been the only way at the time, back when she and the creature had lived as one.

Theo's thumb traced over the back of her hand, a subconscious display of affection. Her eyes flicked down to watch its small circular motions over her skin, and then she felt the ghost of her webs, the thin translucent skin that once stretched between each of her fingers. Theo had touched them, had known them, and still he had not cowered away from her.

For so long she had been apprehensive of his fear, but for the first time Iris wondered if Theo would have ever been capable of fearing her to begin with. She searched his eyes, sifting through their contents for any signs of doubt. All she found was his faith in her, honest and true. It gave her the strength needed for what was to come.

"Nor will I," Iris said with newfound conviction.

***

Iris buzzed with apprehension or excitement. She could no longer tell the difference.

She stood at the window, searching the horizon with observant eyes, while Theo repeatedly paced the length of the cabin the way he did when his nerves got the best of him. The sun was due to peak over the mountaintops at any moment, but Iris had decided to keep Theo in the dark a while longer. She just had one more thing to take care of, she told him, and then they could leave at last.

By the time the first song bird sounded its morning ballad, both Theo and Iris had attained for themselves a deep sense of calm, accepting that whatever might befall them, they would remain as one in heart, mind, and soul.

"Remember, you must do your best to trust me," Iris whispered, sensing that the time was nearly upon them.

"Always."

When Theo once again voiced his concerns about Iris going out on her own, she did her best to reassure him.

"There are still a great many things you do not know of me—things I have, for various reasons, kept from you. But I promise you this—I will tell you all of it once we are on that boat of yours. For now though, you must understand that what I am about to do must be done alone."

Theo could see that Iris was firm in her belief that this was the way things must be. He had promised to trust her, and so trust her he would.

"Whatever awaits you out there, whatever it is you must face, you mustn't forget that you will never be alone so long as I am living. Just utter the word, Iris, and I will be there by your side."

And as morning's golden light crept over the vast expanse of the island, neither of them had ever been more sure of anything. Their love would prevail.

One last embrace and she was gone.

She did not have to search, for the creature was already standing at the edge of the canal, waiting. Iris took her time in her approach, placing one foot in front of the other with the care of one on a leisurely morning stroll. Its lips split upon seeing her.

"He is inside, I can smell him from here. It's just as I expected—you're as selfish as you ever were."

"You misjudge me, but do what you will," Iris replied, her light-footed steps never once lapsing.

It laughed, seemingly unruffled by Iris's composure. "You reek of arrogance, girl. Nobody knows you better than I, for I am you, and you are me."

"The truth will soon reveal itself."

"Yes," the thing hissed. "It will. I believe you will come to rue this moment, my child. What I tried to give you was a chance—the chance to free yourself from the shackles you placed yourself in."

"I've made my choice."

"Indeed, you have. And now you must suffer the consequences."

Iris stood nose to nose with her darkness now, staring into two endless pits of nothingness. She raised her chin in defiance, and in the motion exposed the narrow column of her throat. It seized the opportunity to descend on her then, the many needle-like teeth plunging into her tender, human flesh. The life was being drained expeditiously, out of one vessel and into another. Sweet blood was leached into the very marrow it had once flowed from, and in a few fleeting instants, the mortal body that Iris had invoked for herself had been consumed in its entirety, and it was as if it had never existed at all.

Back in her old skin once more, Iris found she was not alone. The darkness within her persisted, and she struggled in a war against it to reclaim her self. It sought to lay claim to everything Iris was. Claws sunk deeply into her very being. Tearing, ripping, shredding anything it could get its hands on, searching for Iris's softest spots. Her gentleness, her curiosity, her introspection, her feelings for Theo—all of it would all be chewed up and spit out if she did not prevail.

Iris panicked at the thought of these most treasured parts being stolen away from her. And that was when she realized—these things had never been up for taking. There was no set of teeth or piercing talons or a thrashing tail capable of erasing these pieces of herself. She was the only one who had a say in which parts would stay and which would go. And so she chose to keep it all.

Iris took back possession of her endowed savagery, and she kept her carefully cultivated gentleness and curiosity too. All that she'd ever been and would be was once more her own.

She looked down at the stony ground, the brown grass that grew sparsely through its cracks. It was where her human body would have lain if there had been anything left of it. All that remained now was the necklace, the strange pulsing pearl that she'd worn around her neck for a time.

She suddenly had the feeling that it carried a bad omen, and decided to nudge it into the canal where it could return to the sea from whence it came. The moment it touched the water, it began to fizz, bubbling until it dissolved into sea foam. Iris knew not why, but she felt a great pang of remorse as she watched it be carried away.

She then slithered in the direction of the cabin.

"Theo?"

"Iris, are you all right? Is every—" The door swung open and the world seemed to stop. Theo stood in the entryway, frozen with terror.

"You…" His eyes began searching the ground behind her frantically. "Where is she? Where is Iris? What have you done?"

When he rushed at her, Iris clasped him in her arms, easily overpowering his strength.

"No! Where is she? Iris!" he bellowed into the open air. "*Iris!*"

"Stop it, Theo. Can you not see? I *am* Iris."

"No. No you're not. You cannot be." He writhed in her arms. "*Iris!*"

"Stop it, you fool! Did I not express with enough clarity that you would have to trust me? Where is that trust now?"

The tone of frustration in her voice was one he'd heard many times over. He ceased his struggle and looked at her, disbelief written all over his expression. With great care, she took his hand in hers.

"You remember this, don't you?" she asked him.

Something shifted then, and his fear seemed to melt away as they both stood there, reliving the time they'd shared in the caverns. It seemed a lifetime had passed since then, but coming back to it was as easy as breathing.

"Iris?" Theo whispered, not relinquishing his hold on her hand.

She nodded. "Yes."

"This..." He looked at her face, her claws, her eyes. Ran his free hand over the scales on her upper arm, near her shoulder, traced them down to the place where her torso met her tail. She was... different, but she was also the Iris he had known all along. Many things began to click into place in Theo's mind as he regarded her. "This is what you've been hiding all this time?"

She nodded once more. "Yes."

"Why did you not tell me? Why keep it from me?"

"I was afraid, I suppose."

"Afraid of what I would think?"

She said nothing, averting her eyes to his feet. Gently, Theo brushed his fingers over her chin, angling it back up toward him.

"Iris, you've always been the most beautiful thing to me. Nothing about that has changed."

"Really?"

"Really."

An inexplicable sense of giddiness arose within Iris then, effecting a bubbling giggle to rise from somewhere deep within her core. Then they were both laughing, grasping onto each other, clinging to the sweet relief that is complete and utter acceptance. It was a relief so blissful, so intoxicating, that Iris felt the sudden strong inclination to share everything with Theo, to wrench out of herself the parts that brought her the most shame. To bare them to him and ask for his approval, to beg for the absolution that he alone could give her. Only then could things be truly right, truly good.

"And nothing could make you change your mind?" she asked him, a euphoric smile on her face. One that he returned with ease.

As they stood there, basking in their joint ecstasy, Theo gave her his answer. "Not a thing in this world."

And in that moment he had spoken the truth of his heart.

Part Three
Love

Chapter Twenty-Seven

Theo was inside the cabin, alone, pacing once again as if he could outrun his thoughts.

Iris was... He knew not where Iris was, nor did he care at that particular moment. What he needed now was the time and space to wrap his head around her latest confession.

Within the last twenty-four hours, Theo had learned from Iris herself that it was *she* who was responsible for his regrettable fate. *She* who had killed the unconscious Bloody-Eye Bart along with his entire crew just before she stole Theo's limp body from the unforgiving sea and spirited him away to this God forsaken island, this Hell on Earth.

"I had wanted to die!" Theo had exclaimed upon hearing her unbelievable admission. "I threw myself off that ship because I could bear to live no longer!"

Iris, completely taken aback by his anger, responded in kind. "Your death would have been against my will at the time."

"What do you mean by this? What is the reason behind this unfaltering insistence on my living? You slaughtered an entire crew of men just to keep me alive. Why go to such great lengths?"

She shook her head. "I cannot tell you that."

He threw up his arms in frustration. "And why not?"

"Because I no longer wish to! You *assured* me that you would not be angry—"

"I could not have anticipated that you would confess to murder! A murderer who picks and chooses her victims based on—on what? On their taste?" He said it as if the thought were ludicrous, but the silence

STILL WATER

that ensued made him reconsider. "Iris, what do you... What do your kind eat?"

"My *kind*?" She laughed maniacally through her agony. Then she steeled herself, forced herself to look Theo dead in the eye as she said, "*My* kind eat *your* kind."

He did not have to ask her to go, she did that all of her own accord, using her muscled tail to glide gracefully over to the canal, where she sank into its chilling waters without the slightest flinch. And so he was left alone to process this mess that she created.

Before long, Theo's initial outrage subsided enough for him to gain some clarity. He remembered the voice through the window, the things It had said. Now he understood why Iris had pleaded for him not to listen at the time, for if he had, he would've uncovered the truth.

The same truth that she'd just attempted to tell him herself, only to be admonished by him.

He stared out the window in the direction she'd gone, trying to convince himself that the version of Iris that had killed scores of men was also the version that had saved him, that had brought him fish and healing salve when he was sick, that had described to him in great detail the position of the stars on the nights when the sky had been clear, and had listened to him drone on about the cruelties of his father and the deep loneliness he had felt in the Barren Crest.

That very loneliness was one they'd always shared, a common ground upon which they both stood, and on that ground they learned that they no longer had to be alone. Not as long as they had each other.

Theo clung to these thoughts. Willed himself to believe in them. Perhaps under his guidance, Iris could change, could lead a life in which she no longer had to maim or kill ever again. If he could only surrender his love to her, if he could prove to her that it was possible to be forgiven for her trespasses, then she could do it, couldn't she? She could be good.

But the images of death kept flickering through his mind, images that had haunted him since their inception.

Theo went rigid then, his entire body constricting with a new and terrible awareness. He wished he could take back the thought, would have given anything to wring it from his mind, to free himself from this most wicked realization.

Every bit of strangeness that had plagued his life in these past months—it had all followed the disappearance of Clara.

Everything, all of it, began with her.

Chapter Twenty-Eight

Theo's surroundings seemed to fade in and out of focus as he stormed out of the cabin, adrenaline coursing through his veins. His senses took in data—the crisp scent of pine needles, the hazy air, the light drizzle of rain—he was aware of it all, but none of it felt real. He was a flesh-covered phantom, moving mechanically through a world that seemed to unfurl from darkness with his every step. He could not remember at what point he picked up the blade, a filleting knife used for gutting fish, but he could feel the handle's smooth wood chafing against his palm. His footsteps crunched loudly over the brittle grass and somewhere up above a bird let out a sedulous shriek, but beyond that the land was quiet, tentative, holding its breath.

He had to remind himself to stop when he finally reached the canal, lest he walk right into its rushing white waters and be dragged out to sea. Iris was somewhere in those waters, her eyes already upon him, Theo presumed; she was somehow always able to see him, even when he could not see her.

"Iris? Iris, if you've even a shred of decency left you'll reveal yourself this instant. I require a final word before I leave this damned place."

Just as he'd expected, she emerged, eyes animated with something close enough to hatred. The question as to how he could have ever cared for this vile creature flitted through his mind.

"You are leaving?" Iris inquired, her voice suspiciously even.

"Do not pretend you didn't know," Theo said. "Even if neither of us ever said it, I think we both somehow knew it would end this way."

"I suppose I cannot argue with that." Iris's eyes flickered toward the boat, resting only a few feet away from the canal. "Though I think you overestimate your own ability."

"My abilities are my own concern. I care not to hear your thoughts on the matter."

"You may leave only if I permit it, and that is a matter I have yet to decide."

Theo's face flared red. "I do not exist to satisfy your sick and perverted whims. You decide nothing for me."

She laughed gloatingly. In her anger, she came to learn something of love—it is an ugly, selfish thing, and so Iris tightened her grip on her human more than ever before.

"I decide everything for you," she snarled. "From the moment I laid eyes on you, you've been mine. You want to speak of God, Theo? I *am* your God."

Theo took two large steps, submerging himself to his knees in the icy water just so he could glare directly into Iris's eyes. He wanted her to feel the disgust emanating from his body, wanted her to taste his hatred.

"You are nothing," Theo whispered, poison coursing through his every word. "You are no God. You are nothing to me."

Iris lunged at him then, ramming his body out of the canal and into the unforgiving dirt, expelling the air from his lungs. The two of them became a pile of writhing flesh, scratching and tearing and growling like angry beasts. Rage temporarily blinded Iris to her own power and she slashed Theo's face with her claw, carving a long crimson line across his cheek. The sight of it prompted her to withdraw. She leapt away, chest heaving with frenzied pants.

"I *hate* you!" she shrieked, baring her many teeth. And it was the truth. She hated that he lied. She hated that he hated her.

"You hate me, Iris? Kill me then. Kill me like you killed the men on that ship, like you killed Felix. Kill me like you killed all the rest." He was standing before her again, pushing her back toward the water, casting his vicious speech at her like daggers meant to pierce the heart. She slithered backward, away from him, away from the blow she knew was to come.

"*Kill me!*" he bellowed as he'd never bellowed before, bits of spittle flying from his twisted mouth. "Kill me like you killed her! Kill me like you killed *Clara*!"

Iris flinched as if she'd been struck.

"No," he whispered, fingers mashing into her cheeks as he forced her to face him. "You will look me in the eyes when you drain the life from me, Iris."

She did look at him, and that was when she felt the blade pressed against her throat. A bead of blood ran down the steel, dripping onto Theo's clenched hand.

His face contorted into a grimace, teeth bared, eyes welling with tears. His brain begged for him to apply the pressure necessary to end it once and for all, but it was almost as if his hands belonged to someone else; so violently they shook. Iris stood unmoving, arms limp by her sides, face now completely devoid of any resentment or fear. She looked into Theo's eyes, accepting whatever was to come, simply content to be in his arms once more.

Suddenly the blade slipped from his grasp, falling to the ground with a dull thud. Theo collapsed along with it, burying his face in his hands. With a grave sense of horror, he came to understand that his desperate need to avenge his sister's death would live on within him forever. No matter how much he would have liked to plunge his blade into Iris's neck, he simply could not find the strength to do so.

He could not kill Iris.

Theo's lips trembled as he regarded the creature that he loved and hated more than anything else in this world. "Why? Why have you brought me here? Why have you done this to me?"

Iris hesitated.

"You may as well just say it," he said, utterly defeated. "Things cannot become more broken than they already are."

"I had plans of… of eating you."

A hollow laugh. "Of course you did."

"You should know that my mind has long since changed. It seems ages ago that I cast all thought of it away."

"No, you misunderstand, Iris. What you intended for my flesh and bone is not what pains me so. I think I may have even understood it, if you'd have just told me from the start. You were a mere animal, doing what an animal does."

Iris bowed her head as she tried to fight the truth in his words. "I am no animal."

"Yes, you are. But so am I. And so is everyone else. It's quite interesting, Iris, that you find the thought so detestable. Perhaps our fault lies not in the act of existing as animals, you and I, but in our perpetual effort to reach humanness. It is not your nature I resent, but your deception. The entire time you claimed to care for me, you led me to believe in a lie. And that, I have no doubt, came from the most human parts of you."

The dirt on Theo's face was streaked with tears, proof of what he was and what Iris was not.

"I am sorry, Theo." She could think of nothing else to say.

"I…" He looked up toward the sky, releasing a rattling breath. "I fear I am not good enough to forgive you. No matter how I might wish to…" His words came out choked, like the simple act of speaking was now a most excruciating feat.

"Then I will not ask you to," Iris countered, and for the first time in her life, she produced a single tear.

It slid down her cheek, leaving a trail of little salted crystals in its wake. They glimmered faintly, refracting like miniature prisms.

Who could have known that such exquisite beauty could come from such profound pain?

The clouds parted then and the sun's rays intensified, showering Iris in its glorious light. It was a sight that would leave anyone awestruck, and Theo watched in wonder as more tears began to fall from her eyes. One by one, they calcified atop her skin, gradually working to cover the expanse of her body. Theo rose to his feet, concern now prevailing over all other emotions. He frantically attempted to wipe the tiny crystals away, but his efforts were futile. It was as if she were being coated in a shroud of solid diamond.

"Iris, what is this? Please, make it stop," he pleaded.

She smiled, untroubled, an affectionate look in the eyes that she had once despised for their presumed emptiness. Her hand reached out to caress Theo's wounded cheek, and he leaned into it, savoring the softness of her palm before it could be sheathed in the cold, unfeeling mineral.

"Does it hurt?" he asked her, his chest clenching with sorrow.

"No, not at all." She got a far away look in her eyes and placed her free hand over her chest. "I think... I think I can feel it," she said reverently.

"Feel what?" Theo asked, growing more desperate with every passing moment. "Iris, what do you feel?"

Her claws curved inward to pierce her own flesh, reaching into the cavity of her chest. She did not flinch, exhibited no signs of pain. Her hand emerged holding something, a thing small and round. She let it roll into her palm and extended it to Theo.

It was a pearl, just like the one he had found in the palm of the Mourner.

"Take it," Iris said. "Take it so you might feel it too."

He took the pearl into his hand. The moment it touched his flesh it began to flutter.

It was then that Iris understood the true nature of love—it is a flashing, selfless thing, and so finally she let go.

"What is this? Iris, wait! Please, you must tell me. What is it?"

On his knees he begged, but alas, it was too late. Iris had become a shimmering stone, a look of tranquil wonder preserved on her beautiful face for the rest of time.

Besides, Theo hadn't truly needed Iris to answer his questions. He already knew what it was she felt, what it was she had given him. He had known all along. His pleas had been a mere wish to hear her voice one last time.

EPILOGUE

Theo's eyes opened to the faded light of yet another overcast morning. He reached over and stroked the head of long hair that slept beside him. Mercy hummed pleasantly, stretching off the dregs of sleep and turning to smile at her husband.

It was a quiet, tender moment that they shared in the coziness of their bed, but it was short-lived, curtailed by the sound of small feet pattering across the floorboards. Mercy giggled at the ruckus, and ruffled Theo's hair affectionately before sliding out from her place beneath the covers.

"Don't forget, ye promised to help her out in the garden today," Mercy reminded him with a smirk.

"I wouldn't miss it for the world," Theo answered, pulling on a pair of trousers.

And so he ate a quick breakfast before setting off to work under the guidance of Henry Stapleton, who had been kind enough to offer Theo a job in Fort Zenith's shipyard when he miraculously washed up on its shores half-drowned aboard his sea-battered skiff.

After a day's hard work, Theo returned home to his beloved wife and daughter and made good on his promise to lend a hand in the little garden that grew in the front of their humble home.

Theo's life had turned out to be a good one. Simple and without frills, but honest and easy. Good.

He watched as his daughter, now seven years of age, ran over to her treasured bed of flowers. She had been born with a green thumb, an innate affinity for nature and all the living things within it.

Plunging her little hands into the dirt without reservation, she began her task of plucking out the many troublesome weeds. She was so focused, so attentive for one so young. Theo's heart brimmed with pride and love for this child who had given him an entirely new perspective on life. He wondered often over her intuitive wisdom and wit, a trait he thought she must have inherited from her mother.

He had been contemplating all these things, watching her with a wistful expression on his face when she looked up from her chore.

"Can I pick some flowers to put in a vase for Mama?" she asked him.

"Of course. I think she'd like that very much."

She settled on the pretty violet flowers that grew near the back of the small plot. Irises.

"You planted these ones, didn't you Papa?"

He nodded, regarding the freshly plucked flowers and the dirt-caked fingernails with a melancholic smile. "I did."

He bent over to adjust her coat, fastening the top button and smoothing its fur the way he once had many years prior for another little girl. This coat had been on many a journey clutched in Theo's fist, but he was glad for it to once more serve its function of keeping a child warm.

"They're my favorite," she said with her beautiful, naive smile. She brought them to her nose and breathed in their scent.

"I know, my sweet Clara," Theo said to his daughter, his voice growing inexplicably thick. He could hear the whisper of the sea in the distance, an echo of things long since past. "They're my favorite too."

***

The sea's whispers continued on well into the night.

So many questions left unanswered, so many things left unsaid. Perhaps these whispers were trying to tell him something. Perhaps he should heed their call.

Still Water

He slipped out into the crisp night air. A wispy fog laid over the ocean and all was calm, the silver tide gently lapping at his feet.

He felt it in his coat pocket, the faint flutter of the pearl. His fingers closed over it to absorb its perpetual warmth. In the darkness, it seemed to shimmer like the many stars overhead, reminding him of a pair of starry eyes that he had gazed into so long ago.

He clutched the pearl to his chest, closing his eyes so he could focus his senses on the way it quivered. If he concentrated enough, maybe it would reveal what it wished for him to do.

Suddenly, his fingers began to apply pressure. More and more, they pressed down on the pearl's smooth surface until, finally, it cracked. On he pressed, grinding it into a fine dust.

He felt the wind lifting the flecks from his fingers and opened his eyes. Glitter. His fingers were coated in an iridescent glitter that sparkled in the moonlight. Another gust of wind and the rest was swept away.

It swirled in the ocean breeze like a silken scarf, going up and up until he could scarcely see it.

The words tumbled from his mouth before he could comprehend what it was he said, a whisper of his own to match those of the sea.

"Iris, I forgive you."

It very well may have been a mere trick of the mind, but Theo thought he saw the glitter take the shape of a tail just before it vanished from his sight.

www.ingramcontent.com/pod-product-compliance
Lightning Source LLC
LaVergne TN
LVHW041944070526
838199LV00051BA/2903